The Jerry McNeal Series

Port Hope

(A Paranormal Snapshot)

By Sherry A. Burton

The Jerry McNeal Series

Port Hope

By Sherry A. Burton

The Jerry McNeal Series: Port Hope
Copyright 2022

by Sherry A. Burton
Published by Dorry Press
Edited and Formatted by BZHercules.com
Cover by Laura J. Prevost
@laurajprevostphotography
Proofread by Latisha Rich

For more information on the author and her works, please see www.SherryABurton.com

Thanks Mom!

To my hubby, thanks for helping me stay in the writing chair.

To my mom, who insisted I keep the dog in the series.

To my editor, Beth, for allowing me to keep my voice.

To Laura, for EVERYTHING you do to keep me current in both my covers and graphics.

To my beta readers for giving the books an early read.

To my proofreader, Latisha Rich, for the extra set of eyes.

To my fans, for the continued support.

Lastly, to my "writing voices," thank you for all the incredible ideas!

Table of Contents

Chapter One

Jerry gripped the phone, knowing Patti would disappear the moment he answered. "What do you mean help us? I've already helped you and your family find peace. What does Max have to do with this?"

Patti's spirit faded in and out as the phone continued to ring. "Answer it, Jerry. She needs you."

"Are you going to be alright?"

"Help us, Jerry. You're the only one." Patti faded out, reappeared, flickered, then vanished altogether.

Jerry sighed and pressed the button to answer the call.

"Jerry! Thank God you answered. I didn't know what else to do. Jerry, it's the woman from my dreams. She said he killed her!" Max sniffed.

"It's alright, Max. Tell me what you know."

Max sobbed into the phone. "The lady visited me today."

"In your dreams?"

"No. This time, it was different. I was awake. I looked up to see her standing there, staring at me. I tried not to let her know I was scared. She told me to call you."

Mismatch

Jerry ran a hand over his head. "This woman told you to call me? She actually said, 'Call Jerry McNeal'?"

Another sob. "No. She told me to call the man with the dog."

Jerry wanted to think it was a coincidence but knew better. "Okay, Max, I need you to start from the beginning."

"My shoe came untied. I stopped to tie it. When I looked up, the lady was standing there."

"And you're sure the woman was a ghost." As soon as he asked, he knew he'd made a mistake. The sobs on the other end of the phone proved it. Jerry blew out another sigh. "I'm sorry, Max. I know better than to doubt you. It was the cop in me trying to be sure. I believe you, honest I do. Now tell me about the lady."

After a moment, the sobbing eased. "It was her, the woman from my dreams. She had red hair and green eyes just like before."

Patti. But why would she be haunting Max? "Max, did the woman say anything else? Tell you her name, maybe?"

"No, she didn't say her name. I thought it was Virginia, but I'm not sure anymore. She just told me to call the man with the dog. She said you needed to help."

It didn't make sense. He'd already found Patti's body and visited her parents to give them closure.

What else did she expect him to do? And why make a game of it? Why not just tell him outright when she was sitting next to him? *Unless it wasn't her. Don't be ridiculous, Jerry. Of course it's her. Who else?* "So, this woman – this ghost – told you I needed to help her. What happened next?"

"No, she didn't say 'her.' She said 'us.' 'Call the man with the dog. He needs to help us.'" Max started sobbing again. "She said 'us,' Jerry. Why does she think I need help? Please tell me what to do. I'm so scared."

I'm trying. "It's going to be alright, Max. Tell me, this ghost, what was she wearing?" Each time Patti appeared, she was wearing a blue dress. If the clothing matched, it might confirm her to be the woman visiting Max.

"I don't remember."

"Come on, Max, It's important. Close your eyes and try to picture her. Was she wearing a dress?" Jerry waited as silence filled the phone.

Finally, Max spoke. "No, she had on pants and a white shirt. I think it was a sweatshirt. Yes, I'm sure of it. It had a lighthouse on the front, but it didn't look like ours. There was something written on it, but I can't remember what it said."

"That's good, Max. Really good." Actually, it wasn't, as it didn't confirm his suspicion. Not that he would've known what it meant if he'd been right. "Max, does the name Patti mean anything to you?"

"That was the name of your friend you said you were going to visit."

"That's right. My friend Patti was murdered. The thing is, I wasn't going to see her. I was going to see her ghost."

"Oh. I'm sorry."

"Me too, Max. What's more, Patti had red hair and green eyes, and told me I needed to take your call."

"Do you think Patti is my ghost?"

"I think it's a possibility, but I'm not sure."

"I don't understand. Why does she think I need help?"

"I don't know, Max. But I'm going to find out."

"How?"

"I'm going to come to visit you. We'll put our heads together and see if we can figure this out." What he didn't say was that he was kicking himself for not taking the time to help Max when he first realized she was the real deal. If not for Max and her psychic intuition, a lot of people would be dead. Not only Savannah and Alex, but other officers that had no clue how close they'd come to being victims of a deeply unhinged woman. On behalf of all the officers that put their lives on the line every day, Jerry owed it to the girl to help her find peace.

"Really?" Max's voice brightened. "Are you bringing Gunter? I haven't told anyone about him. Not even Chloe, and she's my best friend."

"That's good, Max. Listen, I need to talk to your mom to make sure it's okay that I come to see you. Can you put her on the phone?"

"She's not at home, but I can have her call you."

"Okay, Max. And I want you to do me a big favor. If you see the ghost again, ask her if her name is Patti."

"Okay. I will."

"Try not to be scared. I don't think the woman is there to harm you. I think she's only there because she knows you're special. I'm going to hang up now, Max. After you call your mom, text me your address."

"Okay."

Jerry clicked off his cell phone. Patti had disappeared when he'd answered the phone, but to his relief, Gunter was still there, sitting on the edge of the porch watching a monarch butterfly flutter around the yard. A part of him had worried that the dog – who seemed to enjoy Patti's company – would choose her over him. Jerry pushed off the swing, and Gunter popped up, looking at him expectantly. "Looks like we're going to Michigan, boy."

Gunter jumped up and placed his paws on Jerry's chest, his tail wagging.

Jerry ran his hands through the dog's fur and gave him a pat on the head. "Glad it meets your approval."

Gunter snaked his tongue across Jerry's ear.

Jerry chuckled and pushed him away. "Knock that off before someone sees us and gets the impression I like you."

Gunter growled.

Jerry laughed a full belly laugh. "You know something, dog, it might just be true."

Jerry's cell chimed. He pulled it out of his pocket and saw a message from Max giving him her address in Port Hope, Michigan. *Port Hope sounds like the name of a soap opera or a Hallmark movie, not a place where ghosts hang out.*

"Spirits, Jerry, not ghosts."

Jerry sank the phone back into his pocket and turned to face his grandmother. "Sorry, Granny. How long have you been there?"

She smiled. "Long enough. I'm glad to see you and the dog getting along. I knew you'd grow to like him if you gave him a chance."

Jerry glanced at Gunter, who now sat looking anything but dignified as his hind leg scratched at an imaginary itch. "He'll do."

Granny glanced at his arm. "He didn't mean to bite you, you know."

"I know."

"How is it?"

"Better." He flexed his fingers. "Hand's a little worse for wear."

Granny raised an eyebrow. "That was an expensive lesson."

Jerry shrugged. That he'd gotten angry enough to put his hand through the bathroom mirror didn't bother him so much as the reason. "My only regret is I won't be here to see Savannah's and Alex's faces when they see their new bathroom."

"You could hang around a bit."

"I thought about it for a minute or two. I like how peaceful it is. I heard an owl last night. It reminded me of the one that used to hang out near the house when I was a kid. Slept like a baby after it showed up."

Granny smiled.

"I thought you might've had something to do with that." He decided to take a chance. "I'm going to Michigan. This kid, Max, lives there and is being visited by a ghost. You wouldn't know anything about that, would you?"

Her smile faded. "You know I can't tell you."

He felt his jaw tighten and worked to ease the tension. "I know you believe I need to find my own way, but at least tell me if the kid is in danger."

"You need to go to her, Jerry."

"I'm planning on it." His tone had a bite to it.

"That's enough with the attitude. It doesn't suit you." Granny lifted her hand to his cheek. "I'm glad you came, Jerry. You'll be a better man because of it."

He worked to soften his tone. "It's been a good visit, considering."

Granny removed her hand and smiled a wrinkled smile. "Just remember you're never alone. There are those that can help if you give them a chance."

"What happened to finding my own path."

"Mind your manners, Jerry. You're not too old to be taken over my knee." She laughed as if picturing it. "Receiving help from the living is never frowned upon. Remember, people like you are placed on this earth to help each other, not compete."

"I'll try to keep that in mind." The truth of the matter was he was much better at asking for answers than asking for help.

"I'm always near if you need me." She disappeared before he could answer.

I love you, Granny.

Gunter followed as he loaded the SUV and again as he made a final sweep of the cabin to make sure he hadn't left anything. He placed the key in the drawer and thumbed the card left by the hot neighbor. He sighed, realizing he'd never made time for that beer. *You're a party animal, Jerry. That's all there is to it.*

Jerry had just set his gun bag into the Durango when his cell alerted him to an incoming Michigan call. He closed the door, leaned against the SUV, and pressed connect. "Hello?"

"Mr. McNeal, it's April Buchanan. Max told me what's going on and said you're coming to see her."

"If that's okay with you."

"It's more than okay. This stuff's been going on way too long. Max is not sleeping. She won't admit it, but I can tell from the dark circles under her eyes. She called me a little bit ago and told me she'd just seen a ghost. I didn't want to believe her, but something had her so upset, I could barely understand her."

Jerry wanted to confirm that Max had indeed seen a ghost but decided to wait and do so in person. "I will do everything I can to help Max with this, Mrs. Buchanan."

"Thank you, Mr. McNeal. You don't know how much this means to me."

The desperation in the woman's voice pulled at his heartstrings. "I'll be there soon."

"Thank you. Do you have our address?"

"I do. Max texted it to me after we spoke. I'm driving up from Tennessee. I'll check the Internet to get a hotel."

Laughter drifted through the phone. "I take it you haven't had a chance to Google our address."

That doesn't sound promising. "No, ma'am."

"Our town is about the size of a postage stamp. It's tourist season, and everything is most likely full this time of year. If you don't mind roughing it, my friend Carrie has a camper she keeps at Lighthouse Park for when her parents visit. She already knows the situation and is as worried about Max as I am. She's the one that saw your article in the Gettysburg newspaper and insisted I reach out to you to see if you could help Maxine. Anyway, I'm sure she wouldn't mind letting you use it while you're here."

"That would be much appreciated."

"Good, I'll make sure everything is ready when you get here. And thanks again, Mr. McNeal."

"You're welcome. I'll be in touch with Max to let her know when I get to Michigan."

"Sounds good. Once you cross into Michigan, you'll have about a three- to four-hour drive, depending on how your Navigator brings you. Hopefully, it will be daylight – the lakeshore is a beautiful drive. You'll be able to see Lake Huron just to your right most of the way."

"I look forward to it. I'll see you soon." The call ended, and Jerry looked to Gunter. "Ready for a road trip?"

Gunter jumped up, placed his paws on Jerry's chest, then pushed off, spinning in happy circles.

Jerry raised an eyebrow. "I doubt you'd be this excited if you knew how long of a drive we have ahead of us."

Chapter Two

When Seltzer's number showed up on the screen, Jerry pressed the button on the wheel. "What's happening, Sergeant?"

"How's Tennessee?"

"In my rearview mirror."

"I take it everything is wrapped up."

"We found my friend's body. Actually, it was Gunter who found her."

"Our post sure lost a good trooper when that dog was killed. Glad to hear he's still on the job."

"His job at the moment is riding shotgun with his head through the window." Jerry laughed. "I mean literally through the window – it's rolled up."

Seltzer didn't miss a beat. "Makes for less road noise that way. So, where are you off to?"

"Michigan – I'll be heading up after a quick stop in Indianapolis to check in on a brother." Actually, Doc had mentioned the man during a recent call and asked Jerry if he was in the area to check in on him. Jerry felt obligated to oblige, as he'd failed to adequately warn the guy of the accident he'd seen – a mistake that had cost the man his left leg.

"What's in Michigan?"

"May be something. Might be nothing. Remember the kid I told you about?"

"The one that was dreaming about someone being murdered?"

"That's the one. Her name's Max, and it seems the woman is already dead and scaring the heck out of the kid."

"Sounds like you're the man for the job. Think you can help?"

"The hell if I know. If I can't, I don't know who can. Here's the thing – her ghost has red hair and green eyes."

"Could be a coincidence."

"Could be, but I don't think so."

"Sounds like you've already got a theory."

"I'm hoping that Patti somehow found out that we're connected and is visiting her."

"You don't sound too convinced."

"Max's ghost is wearing different clothes. Every time Patti appeared, she was wearing a blue dress. Max says her ghost is wearing jeans and a sweatshirt."

"It's cold in Michigan."

"Good try, but ghosts don't normally change clothes. I mean, I guess they could, but I've not seen it. The thing is, Patti told me to answer Max's call. She said I needed to help them."

"You think this Max kid is in danger?"

Jerry drummed his thumb on the steering wheel.

"I don't know what to think. I just know Max has helped me out of a jam more than once, and I owe it to her to help figure this out."

"Keep me posted and let me know if you need my help."

"Will do."

"Hey, before you hang up, I forgot the reason for the call. That woman called the station looking for you."

"What woman would that be?"

"That Holly woman from the accident."

Jerry tightened his grip on the wheel. "Did she say what she wanted?"

"Nope. She just asked for your phone number. Of course, I told her we didn't give out the personal numbers of our troopers."

Damn. "Of course."

"Then again, it's not like you're still on the force."

Jerry found himself leaning forward and hanging on Seltzer's every word. "So, you gave it to her?"

"Nope. For all I know, the woman could be a psychopath."

Jerry couldn't tell if Seltzer was being serious or purposely messing with him. "So why tell me this if you didn't give her my number?"

Seltzer chuckled. "Because while I wouldn't give the woman your number, I didn't see any harm in giving her your e-mail address. I figured if she turns out to be a nutjob, you can just ignore her e-mails."

That was Seltzer, always looking out for his best interest. Still, he wouldn't mind if the man had given Holly his number. "Thanks, Sarge."

"Anytime, son. Remember, if you run into any trouble, give me a call."

"I always do." The call ended, and Jerry drummed his fingers on the dashboard. It had been months since Holly's accident. He'd left town under the impression she'd also moved away. If she was trying to get in touch with him, did that mean she'd decided to stay? Jerry sighed. Even if she did, it didn't matter. While he had nothing against Pennsylvania, he had no intention of returning to his old life.

***

"You will arrive at your destination in 500 feet. Your destination is on the right."

Jerry pushed the button to cancel the navigation, checked the address, and turned into the driveway of the brick duplex. He sat staring at the building for several moments before finally getting out and going to the door. His finger hovered just over the buzzer when the inside door opened.

Marine Veteran Tyler Jones, aka Jonesy, stood just inside the door, leaning heavily on a single crutch. His dark hair trailed past his shoulders, and his cheek wore the six-inch welt of a long-healed wound. Heavily tattooed and sporting multiple scars, the man looked nothing of his former self. A fellow Marine, the man would always be a brother, but he and Jonesy had a special bond beyond the brotherhood – Jonesy could also see spirits.

Jonesy unlatched the storm door and pushed it open. "Glad to see you decided to come inside."

Jerry felt the heat rise in his face. "It was a long drive. I was waiting for my circulation to return."

"You don't fool me, McNeal. You're here on a guilt tour. I've told you that you don't have anything to feel guilty about." Jonesy hobbled out of the way to allow him entry. "Nice dog."

Jerry smiled. "I wasn't sure if you'd be able to see him."

Jonesy's mouth dropped open. "You mean he's a ghost?"

"Yep." It still baffled his mind that some people couldn't tell the difference.

"Huh." Jonesy frowned. "I wonder how many ghost dogs I've seen in my life and have never known it."

"Probably more than you realize."

Jonesy moved to the living area. "Want a beer?"

"Sure."

"Cool, they're in the fridge. Bring me one too." Jonesy sank into a recliner and smiled up at Jerry. "I have enough trouble getting around on my own, much less carrying two bottles of Bud."

Jerry found his way to the kitchen, opened the fridge, noted it was well stocked, then took out two bottles of beer. He returned to the living room and handed one to Jonesy. "Nice place you have here."

Gunter took a position where he could clearly see them both and crouched with his hip tilted to the side. Jerry watched the K-9's gaze follow Jonesy's hand as he twisted the top from his bottle and took a taste.

Jonesy traced a thumb around the lip of the bottle. "This is my sister's place. I'm only renting a room. At least for now. She got tired of me feeling sorry for myself and is kicking me out at the end of the month."

Unsure what to say, Jerry took a seat, lifted the bottle to his lips, and took a swig.

Jonesy laughed. "Lighten up, McNeal. I was just messing with you. My sister isn't kicking me out because of my shit. She's getting married. He's a professor at a college in Singapore. Tera's moving over there and taking the kid. I wish you could meet them, but they are off visiting friends, saying their goodbyes before the move."

Jerry knew Jonesy and his sister, Tera, were twins. The man used to talk about her all the time, and every recent conversation had included something about her kid. "That's got to be rough."

Jonesy shrugged. "I'll get by. Tera thinks I'm moping and suggested I get out of my comfort zone."

"Is she right? About the moping?"

"Did Doc call you?" Jonesy leaned forward in his chair. "He did, didn't he? That's why you're here."

Partially. Jerry decided to play it straight with the man. "I called him myself a few days ago. I had some issues of my own and needed to check in. I asked him how everyone was doing, and he said he'd heard from you. I told him if I was in the area, I'd check in to see how you're getting along."

"And you just happen to find yourself here a couple of days later."

Jerry nodded. "I've been in Tennessee for the last few days. I'm on my way to Michigan, and this, as you know, is on the way."

Jonesy frowned. "Tennessee? I thought you were living in Pennsylvania."

Jerry rubbed his hand across the top of his scalp. Though he was happy with his decision, he still wasn't comfortable explaining why he'd left a perfectly good job to strike out on his own. "I was. Not anymore. I left the state post."

Jonesy lifted a dark brow. "I thought you were happy there."

"I was, and then I wasn't. It's no big deal."

"The hell it ain't. You're here trying to fix me, and you're just as screwed up as I am."

"I was. But I think I have my head on straight now." *Maybe.*

"Yeah, why is that?"

"Honestly, I was able to put the past to rest." Jerry held up his hand to ward off questions. "Family stuff, not worth going into. Aside from that, I think getting away from things allowed me to discover my purpose. Maybe that is what we all have to do at some point. Just decompress and get rid of whatever is holding us back."

"You think my sister and her kid are holding me back?"

"I don't know your situation. I was talking about my own baggage. But since you're the one that brought it up, what do you think?"

"I think maybe. Tera doesn't mean to coddle me, but she does, and I let her. At least since the accident." Jonesy held up the beer bottle and smiled. "Sometimes it's easier to let someone else do the work."

Jerry drained the last of his beer and set the bottle on the coaster on the end table. "I wish I would have pushed harder. I knew something bad was going to happen to you. I felt it, and all I did was call and tell you that you might want to reconsider riding your bike that day. I should have insisted that you listen. Made you swear to me you'd stay off the bike for a few days."

"I've told you repeatedly to stop blaming yourself." Jonesy lifted his pant leg to show his titanium leg. "This is on me. You gave me the warning, and I chose to ignore it. You can't save the world, McNeal! But I do need to thank you."

"For what?"

"Saving my life. If not for you, I would have died that day. Because of you, I put on a helmet before getting on the bike. Oh, I always had one with me, but I was too cool to wear it. Maybe cool is the wrong term. I think I thought I was invincible. Yeah, that's more like it. I'd survived multiple trips over to the shit without getting so much as a skinned knee. I liked feeling the wind in my hair, but a bigger part of me felt like I was cheating death each time I returned from a ride in one piece. That day you called, I was like, 'Oh yeah, I'll show him.' I walked to my bike, threw my leg over the seat, and stood supporting the beast with my own two feet. I started the bike, felt the rumble, and decided right at that moment that I didn't want to die. I put on my helmet. No, that's a lie. I kissed the damn thing and said, 'Here's to you, McNeal.'" Jonesy pointed the beer bottle at Jerry and then downed the rest before continuing. "I can still recall everything about that morning, right up until the accident, and then I have a blank space in my memory as if someone cleared the tape. The doctors agree that I would have died if I hadn't been wearing the helmet. What's that old saying? You can lead a horse to water…you warned me not to get on my bike that day. I chose not to listen. But that warning is the reason I'm sitting here right now. As hard as it is to admit, this is on me. Well, me and the woman that ran the red light. She has to deal with what she did. I made my peace with her the day I picked up my check from the lawyer's office."

Jerry had to admit hearing it put like that did give him peace of mind. Especially since the man sitting before him wasn't setting off any red flags. He looked to Gunter to see his response and was pleased to see the dog had grown bored with the conversation and closed his eyes.

He turned his attention back to Jonesy. "So what's next? Are you planning on staying in Indy?"

Jonesy shook his head. "Nope, I'm heading out in a couple of weeks. My sister is selling me her car, and I'm going to drive the wheels off it. Going to see the country and see where life takes me."

Sounds familiar. "Any idea where you'll start?"

Jonesy nodded, pulled out his phone, found what he was looking for, and handed it to Jerry. "I've rented a house in Deadwood, South Dakota for the next six months."

As Jerry looked through the photos, he felt a bit envious of his friend's ability to take off just for the sake of taking off. While technically, he had the luxury of going anywhere he wished, there was always some internal force leading the way. He stopped at the last photo showing dozens of stairs leading from the town to the street above. He looked at Jonesy's missing leg. "Are you going to be able to manage all those stairs?"

Jonesy smiled. "I'll conquer them or die trying."

"If it makes you feel any better, I don't see you dying anytime soon." Jerry winked and handed him back his phone. "I'm sorry this has to be such a short visit, but I have business I need to take care of in Michigan."

Jonesy pocketed the phone. "Any idea where you're going next?"

"Not a clue."

"You find yourself in South Dakota in the next few months, look me up. I'll buy you a beer."

"Thanks, Brother. I might just take you up on that offer." Jerry stood. Gunter popped up and hurried to Jerry's side.

Jonesy pushed off from the chair, and the two men embraced briefly. Jonesy released him and held his gaze. "Tell Doc thanks for looking out for me. That goes for you too, McNeal."

Jerry clamped the man on the shoulder. "You good, Brother?"

"Golden, Bro."

Chapter Three

The drive from the Michigan border to Port Huron was like running a gauntlet of living and freshly mutilated deer. After the eighth near miss of hitting a deer as it ran across the road in front of him, he slowed, leaning forward in his seat in hopes of seeing them before they crossed. In the last ten miles alone, he'd nearly clipped three – during one close call, he was sure he had brushed the doe's tail. He came upon remains in the middle of the road more than once, showing a driver before him hadn't been as lucky. By the time he'd reached the exit to Port Huron, Jerry was ready to be out of the vehicle. He passed a marina on the right and saw the Bluewater bridge to his left, then stopped for the traffic light and checked the navigator. He found a Denny's and pressed go just as the light changed.

It wasn't a long drive, but by the time he arrived, Jerry had had a chance to relax and realized he was more tired than hungry. He glanced at the dashboard and saw it was just after two a.m. Even if he ate and got back on the road, he'd arrive in Port Hope too early to knock on anyone's door. He backed into a parking space near the end of the building, close enough to the door where he wouldn't have to move his SUV when he finally went inside and far enough away to not be bothered by the noise of those dropping in for a bite. Jerry rolled the back windows down enough to get some air without anyone being able to catch him unaware. Not that he was worried about that since Gunter moved to the back seat the moment he lowered the windows.

Jerry cast a glance over his shoulder. "Yo, dog, I'm going to get some shuteye. You've got the watch."

Gunter disappeared momentarily, then reappeared wearing his police K-9 vest.

Jerry reclined his seat. "Good boy. I feel safer already."

***

Sometime before five, Jerry woke to Gunter's low, rumbling growl. Jerry raised his seat enough to see what had gotten the K-9's attention. A black Charger was parked near the entrance of the restaurant. A couple stood beside the car having a heated discussion. Though he couldn't hear what the man was saying, he could tell he was berating the woman. The woman opened the door, and the man reached across her and slammed it once again. The man lifted his hand, and the woman cowered as he backhanded her across the face.

Jerry was on the guy before even realizing he'd gotten out of his vehicle, slamming the man against the side of the car. Gunter was at his side, growling a fierce warning, though Jerry could tell he was the only one who heard the dog. The woman stood just behind him but made no move to interfere. Jerry looked over his shoulder and saw she had tears streaming down her cheeks. The blackish-purple bruise surrounding her left eye let Jerry know this was not the first time the man had resorted to violence.

Jerry nodded to her eye. "He did that to you."

She sniffed and bobbed her head.

"What's your name?"

"Amy."

"Amy, is this your husband?"

Another sniff. "Yes."

"You love him?"

She lowered her eyes and nodded once more. "He's not a bad man. He just loses control every now and then. It's my fault. I was late picking him up for work."

Jerry sighed a frustrated sigh. Why was it women were so quick to absorb the blame for their husband's abuse? "Amy, go on inside and get yourself cleaned up."

She hesitated. "What about Jerry?"

It took a second for Jerry to realize she was talking about her husband. *Shit.* Not only was the guy a jerk, he was soiling a perfectly good name. "Go on inside. Jerry and I are going to have a little

24

chat before we come in. Ain't that right, Jerry?"

The man narrowed his eyes and moved to get away when Gunter clamped down on the man's arm. Jerry smiled and raised both hands for the man to see. "Tell her it's okay, Jerry."

The color drained from the other Jerry's face. "Go on, Amy."

Jerry waited for Amy to go inside the building before motioning for Gunter to release his hold. "You got a middle name, Jerry?"

The man nodded his head.

Jerry sighed. "Well, what is it?"

"Allen."

"Okay, Allen, here's the deal. I'm not really here. I'm a ghost, see. And being a ghost means I can watch you even if you don't see me. You feel a breeze. That's me. You think someone's watching you, also me. You feel someone take hold of your arm when no one's around. Guess who it is?"

Allen just stood there staring.

Jerry popped him alongside his head. "Come on, Allen, try to keep up. You feel someone grabbing your arm. Who is it?"

"You?"

Jerry gave a signal, and Gunter took the man's arm in his mouth.

Jerry smiled a wide smile. "That's right. It's me."

Allen swallowed and looked down at his hand. "But how?"

Jerry lost the smile. "You'd better worry less about the how and more about the why, Allen. Amy said you're a good guy. She seems to think the reason you hit her is because she deserves it. Is that the way you see it?"

"Ye.. ow"

Though Gunter kept hold of Allen's arm, the dog's tail was wagging, and Jerry could tell the K-9 was enjoying the game.

"No, see there, you almost said it was your wife's fault. But we all know that isn't the case, now, don't we?"

Allen nodded his head.

"Good. Now let's see if we can find a better solution. If you get mad at your wife, what should you do?"

Allen stared at Jerry.

Gunter's tail wagged as Allen fell to his knees, batting at his arm as if trying to pull it free from some invisible vice.

"Come on, Allen, you can do better than that. I'll repeat the question: If you get angry with your wife, what should you do?"

"Walk away?" His words were strained.

Gunter released his hold on the arm.

"That's right. From now on, if you get mad at your wife, you'll walk away until you are calm enough to talk to her without raising either your voice or your fist." Jerry doubled his fist and swung at the man, checking his swing just as Allen flinched. Jerry waited for him to recover and then helped him to his feet. "Why'd you flinch, Allen?"

"I thought you were going to hit me."

"And how did that make you feel?"

"What do you mean?"

Jerry grabbed Allen's collar and drew him close. "I mean, how did it make you feel when you thought I was going to hit you?"

Allen gulped, his Adam's apple bobbing up and down. "I didn't like it."

"Yeah, well, you remember that feeling any time you think about hitting your bride." Jerry pulled him even closer. "That's what she is, Allen, your bride. The woman you promised to love and protect."

To Allen's credit, tears formed in his eyes. "I didn't mean to hurt her."

Jerry released his hold. "You're apologizing to the wrong person, Allen."

Allen looked toward the building.

"Go on, but you remember what I said. A bump, a breeze, or a cold chill on a warm day, that's me checking up on you."

Allen bolted across the parking lot without so much as a backward glance. Jerry slapped his chest, and Gunter jumped up. Jerry smiled and ruffled his fur. "You know something, dog. You and I make a pretty good team."

Gunter rewarded him with a doggy kiss.

Jerry ruffled his head once more, then ordered him down. "Come on, boy, I'm in need of coffee and eggs."

A sign just inside the door said to be seated. Amy and Allen were the only other patrons. Jerry positioned himself where he could see their table. Each time Allen looked up, Jerry pointed two fingers at the man and then turned them to his eyes, letting the man know he was watching him.

The waitress approached with a coffee pot and an empty cup. "Coffee?"

Jerry held out his arm. "How about you just start an IV."

The waitress laughed. "From the looks of you, I better make it a central line."

Jerry smiled and ran a hand over his face, feeling the stubble. "That bad?"

She shook her head. "No, I'm just messing with you. I saw you sleeping in your car. I also saw what you did out there."

Jerry shifted in his seat.

"Don't you go fretting yourself. I didn't say nothing. That girl's lucky you had the balls to say something. Not everyone would, you know."

Jerry shrugged. "I'm not everyone."

She filled his cup. "You need a menu?"

Jerry shook his head. "Just bring me some eggs over easy, toast, and bacon."

She smiled. "You got it, handsome."

Amy slid from the booth, and Allen watched until she entered the restroom. Jerry smiled as Gunter walked to the booth and jumped into the seat beside Allen, breathing into the man's face. Allen's eyes grew wide, and he looked across the room at Jerry.

Jerry did the *I'm watching you* thing with his fingers once more, then smiled as the color drained from Allen's face. Gunter stayed next to Allen until Amy returned, then moved away from the man and returned to Jerry's side. Allen shifted in his seat and worked to avoid eye contact with Jerry.

The waitress dropped off food at Amy and Allen's table, then came back, topped off Jerry's coffee, and left him with silverware and ketchup. "It'll be just another minute."

Jerry checked the time on his phone. "I'm not in a hurry."

"I haven't seen you in here before; local or passing through?"

"Passing through. Heading up to Port Hope. You heard of it?"

"Of course. What's in Port Hope?"

Ghosts. "A friend."

"Be careful. The deer will be out."

Jerry laughed. "I've seen enough deer during the night to last me a lifetime. Seriously, the ones in this state are the size of ponies. I must have seen fifty of them between here and Coldwater."

"Must have been a slow night." She winked. "They're bad. I've hit three in three years."

"That doesn't sound good."

"Tell me about it. My husband refuses to get me a new car. He said we've replaced so much on my current car, it's practically new." She topped off his coffee for the third time and looked toward the counter. "I believe your breakfast is up."

Jerry watched as she stopped at the other table, topped off their coffee, then went behind the counter. She returned with his plate and a couple of extra napkins. "Can I get you anything else, Hon?"

Jerry shook his head. "I'm good for now."

She smiled. "I'll check back in a few."

As Jerry ate, the restaurant began to fill with morning diners. Most kept to themselves, a few made small talk with the waitress, and Jerry knew they were regulars. He recalled his waitress at Waffle House and another at the Flamingo, a diner he frequented while living in Chambersburg, Pennsylvania. Now that he'd committed to life as a road warrior, Jerry wondered if he would ever stay in one spot long enough to enjoy that familiar ease of walking into a restaurant and having the waitress know what it was he wished to order.

Allen slid from the booth and headed for the bathroom. He looked over his shoulder several times, making sure he wasn't being followed. Jerry bit his lip, trying not to laugh as Gunter followed him through the door. Jerry pulled his ink pen from his pocket and scribbled his cell number onto a napkin, then walked to the table and handed the napkin to Amy.

Amy held the paper with trembling fingers. "He promised not to ever hit me again."

Jerry held her gaze. "Has he ever made that promise before?"

Tears filled her eyes as she nodded.

"He lays a hand on you again, call that number."

Amy folded the paper and tucked it into her purse.

Jerry had just returned to his table when Allen exited the bathroom. Allen saw him standing at the edge of his booth and froze. Gunter took the opportunity to jump up and place his paws on the man's back. Allen turned, then immediately looked to Jerry, who again did the *I'm watching you* motion. Allen hurried to his booth, but instead of sitting in his original seat, slid in next to Amy.

Jerry thought about changing booths just to mess with the man, then decided against it. The idea was to intimidate the guy into changing his ways, not send him to the loony bin.

Chapter Four

After breakfast, Jerry stopped at at Walmart and purchased a laptop. He hadn't felt the need for one, but that was before finding out he might be receiving e-mails. While he didn't mind using his phone for most things, he decided it might be wise to have a computer if he were going to do any lengthy correspondence. That Holly hadn't even sent him the first e-mail was beside the point. He'd be ready if and when she did.

Max's mom was right: the drive along the lakeshore was most enjoyable. The sunrise on Lake Huron was so spectacular that Jerry pulled over on several occasions just to snap a few photos. While there were deer, most he encountered seemed content to stay away from the road. Refreshing, since he'd yet to drive a full mile without seeing a bloated deer carcass.

Jerry gripped the wheel as a car drifted into his lane and raced toward him at a high rate of speed, only to duck in between the oncoming line of traffic just as Jerry debated veering to the right. It was the third such incident since he'd started up the lakeshore. That people were in a hurry didn't surprise him. That there were no officers staking out this target-rich environment did.

The car in front of him slowed and drifted into the left lane. At first, Jerry thought the driver was in trouble until he realized the guy was merely making a left turn. Jerry looked over at Gunter. "That's an interesting way of doing it."

Gunter didn't seem as impressed as he merely tilted his head.

Jerry stopped at the four-way stop in Port Sanilac. Even though his navigator directed him to go straight, his instincts kicked in, forcing him to make a right. He drove down around the harbor, mesmerized by the sunlight sparkling off the deep blue water like a thousand diamonds dancing along the bay. He circled the loop, turned left, and found himself parked in front of a lighthouse. Though he'd yet to meet Max's ghost, he knew the woman had been here taking photos of the lighthouse. He remembered Max saying her ghost wore a sweatshirt bearing the image of a lighthouse and wondered if this was the lighthouse in question. Maybe, maybe not, but one thing was sure, the woman had visited this very spot.

Gunter whined, sniffed the air, and disappeared. Jerry heard a bark and looked to see the dog sniffing at the base of the weathered fence. Either the dog had gotten a whiff of another K-9, or he too had picked up on the energy. Jerry thought it to be the latter as Gunter now stood with his paws on the picket fence, looking longingly at the lighthouse beyond. Jerry pulled out his phone and took a picture, then a second, zeroing in on the spot where the dog stood. He checked the photos even though he knew before looking that the dog would not show. He was right, of course. The image merely showed the fence that surrounded the structure. The groundskeeper's house was red brick, connected to a white lighthouse that jutted high into the cloudless sky. Jerry saw a sign attached to the fence and got out to take a closer look. Crossing the road, he took a photo of the sign, which stated that the Port Sanilac Light Station was constructed in 1886, gave further stats regarding the lighthouse, and further stated the lighthouse was now privately owned, and therefore not open to the public. Though the sign stated no one was allowed to enter the grounds, Gunter pushed through the fence and materialized unscathed on the other side, wagging his tail and looking rather pleased with himself.

Jerry chuckled. "Showoff."

Gunter barked and lowered into a playful bow. He bit at the grass, tossing it over his head, his tail wagging as if begging Jerry to join him in his escapades.

Jerry shook his head. "Yeah, I don't think so. You get locked up, you can walk through the bars to escape. I would stay in the cell until my arraignment."

Gunter answered by dropping to the ground and rolling on his back.

"I've had enough sightseeing. Let me know when you're ready to continue." Jerry turned and headed back to his Durango, talking loud enough for Gunter to hear. By the time he opened the driver's door, Gunter was sitting in the passenger seat waiting for him.

Jerry followed the road, made a right at the stop sign, and another right back onto M25. He stopped at the same four-way stop, proceeding straight through the intersection.

Slowly, the landscape began to change, showing small hills within the terrain. Jerry admired some of the houses nestled along the waterfront and wondered at their morning view of the sunrise over the water. *A person could get used to that. Then again, it probably sucks in the wintertime.*

As he continued up the lakeshore, Jerry noticed enormous black birds gathering in the trees. Intrigued, he waited until there were no cars in either direction and stopped in the middle of the road, staring at a tree that held at least a dozen of the large birds. He blew his horn, and Gunter barked as the birds took flight. *Not blackbirds, buzzards* – flocks of them. While he'd occasionally seen a few circling overhead, Jerry had never seen so many in one place. Though the sky was clear, the sight of numerous buzzards doing lazy circles over the shoreline lent a slightly ominous feel to the air.

As Jerry continued, he came to another town. Though the massive water tower sported the name Sand Beach, the sign on the outskirts of town read Harbor Beach – further proclaiming it to be the world's greatest man-made harbor. Though still a small town, it was the largest he'd driven through since leaving Port Huron. There was a vast brick building to the right with what looked to be a hand-painted mural. Two paintings stood out: one with a steam train and the other with a lighthouse. Jerry's intuition told him that the woman visiting Max had stopped to gather photos of this as well. The second he pinged on the lighthouse, the hair on the back of Jerry's neck began to crawl. He turned to Gunter. "She was a tourist."

Jerry took a right and drove to the water's edge, knowing she too had taken this route – and had sat looking at the lighthouse. This one sat out on a spit, so he could only admire it from afar. He wondered briefly if there was a way to get closer, then decided it didn't matter. What he was looking for was not here. After a moment, Jerry let off the brake and drove back to M25 to continue on his way.

He'd no sooner turned back onto the main road when Gunter barked. Jerry looked to see what had gained the K-9's attention. On the porch to the left were what looked to be large wooden carvings of a pirate and a sea captain.

"It's okay, boy; there's nothing to worry about. They're not real." Jerry looked at his ghostly companion and laughed at the absurdity. He glanced at his image in the rearview mirror. "McNeal, I do believe you're losing your mind."

Just past the city limits, a car pulled out in front of him. Instead of speeding up, the vehicle appeared to lose speed until it was doing well under the posted speed limit. Jerry pressed on the brake to keep from rear-ending it. Just as he decided to go around, the car drifted into the other lane. *Great, another Michigan left*. Jerry started to lay on the horn, then realized the hair on the back of his neck was tingling even more than before. He craned his neck to look inside the car as he drove past and saw the driver hunched over the steering wheel. *Shit!* Jerry wheeled the Durango around and pulled in front of the car, which had come to a stop in the drainage ditch.

Jerry jumped out of the Durango and ran to the man's car and opened the door, which was thankfully unlocked. The man had snow-white hair and a bushy white mustache, which appeared even whiter given his lips were an eerie shade of blue. He was sweating and clutching his left arm. Jerry helped him lean back against the seat, pulled his cell phone from his pocket, and dialed 911.

The call was immediately answered. "911, what is your emergency?"

"I am just north of Harbor Beach on M25 with a man who appears to be in his early seventies, and I suspect he's having a heart attack." Gunter barked, and Jerry looked to see buzzards circling overhead. *Damn, they didn't waste any time.*

"Is the man breathing?"

"At the moment." Jerry looked at the birds, wondering if they knew something he didn't. "His lips are blue."

"Stay on the line, sir. Help is on the way." The dispatcher had no sooner said the words than Jerry heard sirens.

Got to love a small town. Then again, Jerry remembered seeing the signs for the hospital, which was probably close enough he could have carried the man himself.

A Harbor Beach sheriff's vehicle was on the scene within two minutes of his call. A tall, lanky officer jumped out and raced to the car. "Hershel?"

The man's eyes fluttered.

The officer keyed his mike and relayed the man's name to the dispatcher. His face was grim as he spoke to Hershel, letting him know help was on the way. The officer looked at Jerry, "You from around here?"

"No, sir. I was on my way to Port Hope when I saw him drive off the road." Jerry purposely left out the part of Hershel pulling out in front of him. "He a friend of yours?"

The officer laughed. "More like a friend to the whole town. Hershel here is the father of one of our firefighters. He's lived in this town his whole life, ain't that right, Hershel?"

Hershel moaned his answer through gritted teeth.

Within moments, the road was filled with those who either were there to help or who'd heard the call and personally knew the man. Aside from the heart attack, Jerry found himself envying Hershel, who was obviously not only well known but well-liked. By the time they took the man away, it seemed as if everyone in town had personally shaken Jerry's hand and thanked him for his good deed.

It was after ten before Jerry left the scene. He'd barely driven a mile when he saw what looked like chickens standing at the side of the road. As he neared, he realized they were not chickens but turkey vultures feasting on a fresh deer carcass. Jerry looked up, not surprised to see buzzards circling overhead. He turned to Gunter. "If anything happens to me, promise you won't let them near me."

Gunter growled and licked his lips.

Jerry laughed. "I don't know if that makes me feel better or worse." He pressed on the gas, the noise from the Hemi engine scattering the birds momentarily. He'd no sooner passed than they returned to their task of picking the carcass clean.

Jerry passed a campground on the left and wondered if that was where he'd be spending his evenings. He noted a small restaurant with a sign that said "Pirate's Cove" on the opposite side of the road. The parking lot was full, so Jerry assumed the food was worth eating.

As he neared Port Hope, Jerry felt that familiar pull. Even if Max hadn't told him of her dreams, he would have known something was off in the otherwise sleepy little town. The only way to explain the feeling was that of being watched, and so far, Jerry had not seen a single soul. Even as the navigator alerted him of his arrival, he knew he'd yet to reach his destination—the ghostly energy that pulled at him and begged him to fix the wrongs.

The town was called Port Hope – he'd learn later that it wasn't actually a town but a village that was home to around two hundred residents. The sign on the outskirts of town proclaimed it the "little town with the big welcome." No buzzards were flying overhead – no vultures dining on things left to rot along the side of the road. And yet something was not as it should be. That something hovered in the air and begged him to take notice.

.

Chapter Five

When April had told him that the town was the size of a postage stamp, she wasn't kidding. Jerry was able to drive the length of it in less than two minutes. He ignored the navigator's cues to turn, as he wanted to get a feel for the town to try and figure out why his paranormal senses were pinging on the otherwise normal-looking town. It was small but not unlike many of the other Michigan towns he'd passed along the way. There were cars parked along the street and a few people milling about, none of which set off any warning bells.

Jerry reached the city limits, did an exaggerated U-turn, and made a second pass through town, making a mental note of the small post office, mercantile, and a few other shops on the east side of the road. A two-story orange brick building to his right sported the name Port Hope Hotel. The building looked as if it had been there for at least a hundred years, and upon further inspection, it appeared to be more of a restaurant than a place that welcomed overnight guests. Multiple beer signs hung over the wooden porch rail, including one that said they had beer on tap. The sign out front said

"Port Hope Hotel, home of the Leroy burger." Jerry added it to the list of things to try while in town.

Across the street was a small two-pump gas station. Jerry continued south, making a left and turning around in the city municipal building parking lot. He noted a small block building, with a two-tone brown brick front, topped with a red and white awning. The sign simply proclaimed it to be "The Store." Since he hadn't noticed any stores other than the combined mercantile/hardware, the name seemed fitting. The fact that a beer truck was currently unloading at the back of the building was also a plus.

Satisfied with his preliminary tour of the town, Jerry followed the navigator to a white two-story house located in the center of the village. There were no cars in the driveway, but he could see what looked like a note taped to the front door. He got out, went to the front door, and checked the note. Sure enough, it was an envelope with his name on it. Jerry opened it and found directions to the campground, the lot number, along with a key to the camper. *Must be a safe town if she didn't have to hide the key.* Upon reading further, the note told him to text April when he was settled, and she would pick up Max early from school.

Jerry heard someone sneeze and saw an older woman working in the yard next door. She was wearing yellow gloves and an oversized sun hat. He instantly thought of his granny, as the woman loved working in her flowerbeds and often insisted Jerry join her. He didn't mind, since his grandmother was full of stories and had a knack for making even the most arduous task seem fun.

The woman looked up from her weeding and saw him watching. She removed her hat and drew a cloth from her apron, and wiped her face. "You must be Jerry."

That she knew his name caught him off guard. "Yes, ma'am."

She was kneeling and placed her hands on her knees. "Max told me you were coming. A troubled soul, that one. She told you she saw the woman, did she?"

"Yes, ma'am."

The woman looked to make sure no one was listening before continuing. "April doesn't believe her, but I do. I saw the truth in her eyes when she told me. The child was scared, and it wasn't an act. She saw something, and that's all there is to it. She said you can see them too – ghosts, that is. Said as how you're coming here to help her figure out what the woman wants."

Jerry shifted his weight. "Yes, ma'am."

"You don't say much, but at least you're polite about what you do say." The woman raised her hand and batted at an unknown intrusion. "Dang gnats are out early today."

Her gnat was a ninety-pound ghost dog who'd just sniffed her ear and was now in the process of watering the woman's irises with an invisible stream. Jerry clapped his hand to his leg in a bid to get Gunter's attention. "Yes, ma'am, I feel them over here as well."

The woman returned her hat to her head. "Strange, they're not normally out this early in the day."

Jerry stifled a smile and returned her wave as he headed back to his SUV. He opened the door, and Gunter sailed in ahead of him, taking his place in the passenger seat. The woman turned from her task and waved to him a second time as he drove away, the gesture once again reminding him of his grandmother.

The campground ended up not being the one he'd passed along the way. He turned left onto M25 and continued north up the coast. The second he made a right onto Lighthouse Road, the hairs on the back of his neck began to prickle. He rounded the bend and saw the campground to his right. There was no entrance on this side, so he followed the road until he saw the sign for Lighthouse Park.

The lighthouse loomed ahead of him, a white brick building attached to a matching lighthouse. Instead of warning him away from danger, the energy that surrounded Pointe Aux Barques drew him forward. Though the pull was great, Jerry knew the spirits that beckoned were from souls that had long passed. Whatever brought him here had seen fit to involve Max. It wouldn't be fair to the girl to start without her. Furthermore, if he was going to help the spirits, he needed to set some ground rules. The first order of business, attend to his basic needs, which meant checking out his accommodations.

Jerry turned right and followed the dirt road past the opened gate into the campground, then used the note to find the camper. The campground was about half full, with many of the campers looking as if they'd been parked in the same spot for years. He pulled up to the campsite and checked his note to make sure he was in the right place. When April asked if he minded roughing it, he envisioned a small popup camper, not the newer black and white fifth wheel camper that sat on a campsite closest to the lake. Jerry looked over at Gunter. "I hope the weather cooperates. With this location, we're apt to see some spectacular sunrises."

Gunter yawned his enthusiasm. Jerry laughed and ruffled the dog's fur. "At least check it out before you pass judgment."

Gunter jumped out after him, sniffed the air, and wagged his tail.

Jerry smiled. "Glad it meets with your approval."

The inside of the camper was even nicer than the outside, with all the luxuries of an upscale apartment, including a tiled shower, designer kitchen with an island, and full-size gas range. Jerry looked out the window at his Durango and, for the first time since purchasing it, regretted his decision. "Yo, dog, what do you say we trade our ride in on a pickup truck and get ourselves one of these?"

Gunter tilted his head and wagged his tail.

Jerry went back to the Durango to get his bags. He wondered how many keys to the camper were floating around, debated on leaving his gun bag in the SUV, then decided against it, making a mental note to take the bag with him whenever he left. He hoisted the seabag over his shoulder, then picked up the gun bag.

"I haven't seen you around here before. Are you renting the camper from Carrie?"

Jerry turned toward the voice and saw an older gentleman with grey hair coming around the front of the camper next to the one he was using. The man wore loose-fitting jeans and a checkered shirt with sleeves rolled to the elbow. He walked to a blue Adirondack chair – the back of which was shaped like a mitten – sat down with a grunt, leaned forward in his chair, and used a stick to poke at the smoldering firepit.

Jerry firmed his grip on the gun bag and nodded. "Carrie's a friend of a friend. She's letting me use the camper."

The man eyed the gun bag. "Staying long, are ya?"

Jerry almost told him it was none of his business but didn't want to get off on the wrong foot. "A few days, more or less."

Gunter moved past the man, and Jerry positioned himself to see the dog, who'd placed his front paws on the steps of the guy's camper and stood with his head pressed through the middle of the door. Gunter's tail was erect, and Jerry wondered what had caught the K-9's attention. A deep bark from inside the camper gave him his answer.

"Quiet, Lady!" The man turned to Jerry and raised an eyebrow. "Lady's in heat. You don't own a dog, do you?"

"No, sir." Jerry looked to Gunter, whose body was now halfway through the closed door. It wasn't a lie. While the dog chose to travel with him, technically, Gunter did not belong to him or anyone else. Gunter was a ghost – a K-9 spirit who'd attached himself to Jerry a few months back. Legally speaking, being haunted did not qualify as owning the spirit. *Jesus, Jerry, you need some sleep.* Jerry turned toward his camper.

"I saw you pull in and didn't know if you had a dog with you, so I put Lady inside just to be safe. Glad you don't have a dog, or I'd probably have to keep her inside the whole time. The name's Jeff Mills. I'd get up and shake your hand, but I see they're full. You need anything, just ask. My wife and I can either get it for you or tell you where to find it. We've lived in the area all our lives. We've gotten old and now spend the winters in Florida, but Edith doesn't like being away from the grands that long, so we head north the moment the frost ebbs."

"Jeff, come quick. There's something wrong with Lady."

Jeff pushed off the chair and hurried to the camper door. Jerry opened the door of his own camper and slid his bags inside before walking over to see if he could help.

Jeff was standing just outside the open door, and a woman Jerry presumed to be Edith stood just inside. Edith wore a light pink sweatsuit even though the weather was warm. Her eyebrows appeared to be drawn on, and Jerry instantly felt that she was unwell.

The woman saw Jerry and her hand went to her head as if checking to see if her hair was in place. Satisfied, she turned her attention back to the dog. "Look at her. She's just standing there. I told her to lie down, and she just looks at me."

Jerry craned his neck to see inside and saw a beautiful German shepherd standing in the middle of the living area. Smaller than Gunter, she was stunning in that her coat was shiny and black. The dog stared at him with dark, searching eyes. Jerry leaned in further and saw the reason Lady wasn't moving was because she couldn't – not at the moment anyway. Gunter stood behind her, facing the opposite direction, held together by an appendage only Jerry could see. It never occurred to Jerry to question whether Gunter had been neutered. That he wasn't was quite apparent given the display before him. *Shit!*

Jeff clapped the side of his leg and tried to coax Lady outside.

Lady walked in circles, taking Gunter with her as she moved. If not for the confusion on the dog's face and the fact that he was the only one that knew of Lady's current predicament, Jerry would have found the situation extremely amusing. *Think, Jerry.* He cleared his throat to suppress the laughter that threatened. "You know, I had an uncle who once had a dog act like that. It happened every now and then when the dog came into heat. The only thing that worked was to leave her alone for a bit of time."

Jeff scratched his head. "Your uncle's dog, did they find out what was ailing her?"

Jerry groped for an answer. "Pseudo K-9 arousal or something like that. It comes on when the dog thinks another dog is near and they are waiting for a connection." *Jesus, Jerry, do you think they're actually going to buy that?*

Jeff's gaze swept over the campground. "I guess that makes sense. There are other dogs around."

Edith twisted her hands together. "So, what, we just leave her in here?"

"Yep, give her a little privacy, and she'll be

good to go in no time." How Jerry managed to keep a straight face, he didn't know. He also didn't know if Gunter was capable of impregnating the dog. If he did, would they be normal earthly puppies or half dog, half ghost? Unfortunately, Jerry would be long gone before he had a chance to find out.

Jeff returned to his chair, but Edith decided to keep Lady company until she snapped out of her presumed trance.

Jerry bid them both goodbye and returned to his camper alone. The breeze coming in through the open windows was cool and welcoming. Jerry yawned and rolled his neck. He'd only gotten a few hours of sleep and was in need of a little more if he was going to be on his game. He looked longingly at the king-size bed, centered at the back of the camper with a window just above. The bed called to him like a siren's beckon.

Jerry ran a hand over his head and opted for the recliner instead, knowing full well if he stretched out in bed, he'd still be there come morning.

Jerry closed his eyes, recalling the day's events: the drive through deer central, the encounter with Allen and Amy, and his being there at just the right time to help save Hershel's life. While a part of him missed having a place to call home, a larger part of him enjoyed the satisfaction of helping people just because he was in the right place at the right time.

Chapter Six

A mist appeared in the corner of the room, and Max held her breath as it transformed into the woman who'd been haunting her dreams. Max started to run, remembered Jerry asking for her help, and squared her shoulders.

"Maxine? Did you tell him?" The woman's words came out as a whisper.

"Yes, I told him." Max hated when people called her by her given name, as it made her feel as if she'd done something wrong. "I've told you before, my name is Max."

"Max is a boy's name. You don't want people to think you're a boy, do you?"

"Of course not. Max is short for Maxine. I just like the way it sounds. Is your name Patti?"

The woman frowned. "No, why would you think that?"

"I told my friend Jerry you have red hair, and he wanted me to ask you if your name is Patti."

The woman crossed her arms. "Not all redheads are named Patti."

"I know. His friend had red hair, and she's dead. I guess he thought you might be her."

"This friend, he's the one you told me about?"

"Yes, Jerry. He's a cop. Well, not anymore, but he used to be."

"Why isn't he here? I thought you told him to come." Though she was still whispering, the woman seemed upset, and the energy that surrounded her frightened Max.

"I did. He promised he would come."

The woman narrowed her eyes. "I want him here now."

Max took a step back. "He's not a ghost. I can't just make him appear."

The spirit moved closer. "I need to speak to him."

"You're scaring me. You need to leave."

"I can't leave. Don't you understand?"

Max took a breath. "Is it because you were murdered?"

The spirit's hand moved to her throat.

Max remembered what Jerry said about needing more information. "Who did that to you?"

"The man."

"Did you know him?"

"I'd met him before."

"What was his name?"

"John. John Smith." The woman closed her eyes and rubbed her hands along her arms. When she opened her eyes again, her energy was even darker than before. "I'm tired of being questioned by a child."

Max was incensed. "You're the one that came to me."

The woman whirled on her, pressing her boney fingers into the tender flesh that connected her arm to her shoulder. "That's because you're the only one who can see me."

"I didn't ask to see you." Max blinked back tears. "You're hurting me!"

"Max, honey. Wake up. You're having another bad dream."

Max opened her eyes, relieved to see her mother sitting on the side of her bed.

Max sniffed and brushed her hair from her face.

Her mother moved a strand that she'd missed. "Was it the lady?"

Max nodded her head. "She's mad Jerry's not here yet."

"It was just a dream."

Max still felt the pain from where the woman grabbed her shoulder. "It didn't feel like a dream."

Her mother sighed. "Jerry should be here today. I'm sure he will help you figure this out."

"And if he doesn't?" Max wanted to believe he could help, but he didn't seem to be all that good at figuring things out on his own.

Her mother kissed her on the top of her head. "We will cross that bridge when we come to it."

Max knew that was her mother's standard

answer when she didn't know what else to say.

April fluffed Max's pillow. "You need to get some sleep. Do you want me to leave the light on?"

Max wanted to tell her she wasn't a baby, but at the moment, she didn't mind being treated like one. "Yes, please."

Her mother kissed her on the cheek then stood. "I'll leave the door open. If you need anything, I'm right down the hall. Okay?"

Max nodded.

Her mother paused at the door. "He will be able to help. I just know he will."

Max pulled the covers close and turned to face the wall. It wasn't that she didn't believe her mother. It was just because she didn't want her mom to see her tears. *Jerry has to help. He just has to.*

***

The rest of the night remained uneventful. It had taken a while, but Max was finally able to drift off to sleep. Now with the sun filling the room, she second-guessed herself, wondering if the visit had, in fact, merely been just a dream. She got up, started dressing for school, and noticed a tenderness that hadn't been there the day before. Max went to the mirror and pulled back her shirt, exposing her shoulder. Her breath caught as she saw a fingerprint bruise in the exact spot where the woman had grabbed her. *It wasn't a dream! Mom will have to believe me now.* Max started off to find her mom, then hesitated. *No, she won't. She'll think I got into another fight at school and accuse me of making the whole thing up. She'll probably even think I was faking my nightmare.* Okay, so that was partly her own fault as she had acted out on occasion, but this time, she was telling the truth. Max heard her mom coming and straightened her shirt so she wouldn't be able to see the bruise.

April looked her up and down. "Feeling better today?"

The concern in her mother's voice almost made Max reconsider her decision. Almost. "Uh-huh."

"Any word from Mr. McNeal?"

Max was so caught up in the events of the night, she'd completely forgotten to check. She went to the dresser and brought up her messages. Sure enough, there was a text from Jerry. She read the message and smiled to hide her disappointment. "Jerry said he had to stop and get some sleep. He won't be here until around lunchtime."

"I'll tell you what. I'll leave Mr. McNeal a note and tell him to let us know when he gets settled, and I'll pick you up from school early."

Max's disappointment dissipated. "Really?"

"Yes, really. The sooner we get this mystery solved, the sooner we can get some real sleep. Now, finish getting ready. I have to run to Bad Axe to do some shopping, and I'll drop you off at school on my way."

"Or I could just go with you...you know, since you're going to let me leave early anyway." *Unlikely but worth a shot.*

Her mother laughed. "Nice try. Now hurry and get ready."

Max couldn't believe her luck. Not only was she finally going to meet Jerry, but she was getting to come home early, which almost never happened. Max waited for her mom to leave the room, then checked her shoulder, half expecting the bruise to be gone. It wasn't. *Just wait until I show Chloe.*

She'd not shared her abilities with all of her peers, but Chloe knew everything. Well, not everything, because Max had never told anyone about Jerry's dog. Oh, she'd been tempted a time or two, but in the end, she'd promised Jerry she wouldn't tell.

Chloe thought it was cool, her seeing ghosts and all, saying most people had to pay to go to the movies and further telling Max she was lucky because she had them in her head. Max didn't think they were so cool and wondered if Chloe would change her mind when she saw the bruise. *Probably not.*

Max put her hand on her shoulder, wondering what Jerry would say. She would tell him about the bruise, but she hadn't told him everything. Like when the woman told her some of what the man did to her. Max didn't even want to think about those things, much less tell anyone. She hadn't even gotten the courage to tell Chloe. Max told her that the woman couldn't speak above a whisper but left out that the lady's lack of voice had something to do with the bruises around the woman's neck. She also hadn't told Chloe those bruises scared her more than the woman's presence, as they were shaped like fingerprints, or that someone had killed her, mainly because Max knew she'd been killed right here in Port Hope.

Max thought that just maybe if she didn't say it out loud, it wasn't real. This was Port Hope, not Detroit. Bad things didn't happen here. That was why she and her mother had settled here after her mother's divorce. The problem was, as much as she wanted to believe it wasn't true, she'd seen the evidence to prove otherwise. Evidence which now visited her in her dreams each night and left telltale marks on her shoulder. That would be over soon now that Jerry was coming. At least, she hoped that was true—a part of her worried that he wouldn't be able to fix the problem, mostly because things didn't add up. The article that her mom's friend, Carrie, had given to her mom said that Trooper McNeal was an asset to the Pennsylvania State Police Post – stating that Jerry's gift of intuition helped him save lives, fight crime, and in many cases, stop it even before it happened. That was part of what Max didn't understand. If he could fight crime and had people who believed him, why did he quit being a cop? If she had a job like that, she would never leave, especially if her boss believed her. It just didn't make sense to her, and for that reason, she was afraid to get her hopes up. Still, she was looking forward to finally meeting Jerry and telling him everything she knew. *He will believe me. He just has to.*

***

The last bell rang, and Max hurried from class, hoping to meet her mom without being seen. No such luck. Chloe joined her before she'd even reached her locker. "What are you still doing here? I thought you were leaving early."

Max shrugged. "Jerry never texted."

"Do you think he ditched you?"

"No!" At least, she hoped not. At first, she'd gotten angry at him for not answering, but now she was getting worried since he'd yet to answer her texts. "It's not like him not to answer."

Chloe matched her steps. "Do you think something happened to him?"

Yes. "I don't know."

Chloe hesitated when Max stopped at her locker. "I'll save you a seat on the bus."

Max shook her head. "Mom's picking me up."

"Okay."

Max tugged her backpack onto her shoulder and winced when the strap pulled at the bruise.

Chloe frowned. "Does it hurt much?"

Max shrugged. "Only when I touch it."

Chloe looked toward the entrance. "I really hope Jerry shows up and helps you get rid of the ghost. I thought it was cool at first, but not if she's going to hurt you."

Max smiled at her friend. "Thanks, Chloe. Now go before you miss your bus."

Chloe gave her a quick hug before running toward the loading area. Max shut her locker and then slowly walked to meet her mom.

April raised an eyebrow when Max slumped into the seat. "Looking pretty glum there, kiddo. Rough day?"

Max resisted the urge to roll her eyes. "Jerry never showed up, and you didn't get to pick me up."

April laughed. "What do you call this?"

"MOM, you know what I mean."

"Watch your tone, young lady." Her mother curtailed her own tone. "I know what you mean, but I'm here now, and so is Mr. McNeal."

Max sat up in her seat and strapped on her seatbelt. "You talked to him?"

April checked the side mirror before pulling away from the curb. "No, but the note with the key is gone. No one else would have taken it."

Max wanted to argue that point but didn't want to upset her mother by letting her know they had a possible murderer on the prowl. "Can we go see him?"

"I think we should wait until he calls."

"Mom, it's not like Jerry not to answer my texts. What if something's wrong?"

April sighed her resignation. "Fine, we'll go check on him just to make sure he's okay."

Jerry was okay. Max would have felt it if he weren't, but that was what bothered her. Why would he take the trouble of driving all the way there and not check in once he arrived? The question was just another piece of the puzzle that had her questioning whether Jerry was the right person to help her. She'd pinned all her hopes on the man and now he didn't have the decency to call. She knew she was judging him unfairly, but he was a guy, and guys were not to be trusted.

Chapter Seven

Jerry heard a car door slam, then another, followed by a knock on the camper door. He checked the clock over the microwave and realized he'd been sleeping for nearly five hours. He opened the door to find Max and her mother, although April looked young enough to be the girl's older sister. Both had the same slim build, the same mousy brown hair that hung just below the shoulders, and while April looked happy to see him, the frown on Max's face told him she did not share her mother's enthusiasm.

April scanned the length of him and smiled. "Mr. McNeal, I'm April, and this sourpuss is Max. I'm glad you were able to make it."

"It's Jerry. Please come in." Jerry moved back to allow them entrance. Max's lack of smile baffled him. Her texts always seemed so bubbly. He smiled at her. "What's got you in such a sour mood?"

Her eyes grew wide, and then she recovered. "Nothing."

April cocked her head. "Maxine Buchanan, you have something to say, out with it."

Max's face turned red. "Mom."

April squared her shoulders. "If you won't tell him, I will. Max was expecting you here by lunch. I told her when you let us know you were in town that I would pick her up from school."

Jerry ran his hand across his head. "I am so sorry. I didn't get much sleep last night. I came in, felt the breeze coming off the lake, and thought I'd close my eyes for a couple of minutes. I didn't wake up until I heard the car doors."

Max's lips trembled. "You said you were stopping for the night to sleep, and that's why you wouldn't be here this morning."

Jerry sighed. The last thing he wanted was to upset the girl. "I sent you that text last night because I knew if I told you I was coming in during the night, you would wait up for me and not get any sleep. I drove through to Port Huron, then grabbed a couple of hours sleep in the Denny's parking lot."

Max stared at him for a moment. "Is that where you got in the fight?"

April's eyebrow went up. "You got in a fight?"

Jerry shook his head. "I didn't get in a fight. I stopped one. It was a domestic – between a husband and wife."

A look crossed between April and Max, and April nodded her head. "Did you stop it?"

"I did."

April rubbed her arms. "Good."

Jerry moved his bags out of the way and waved

them toward the living area. "I'm sorry. Please have a seat so we can talk."

April wasted no time making herself comfortable. Max took her time looking about the camper as she moved to the living room. April kicked off her shoes and tucked her feet up under her. "Is the camper to your liking?"

Jerry smiled. "When you said roughing it, I was thinking something less luxurious than this. To tell you the truth, it is nicer than my last apartment. Substantially bigger too."

April laughed a carefree laugh. "It's nicer than our house as well."

"There isn't anything wrong with our house." Max crossed her arms and glared in Jerry's direction.

April tossed Max the keys. "Max, run out to the car and get my water bottle."

Jerry looked toward the kitchen area. "I haven't checked the fridge yet. There might be some water in the fridge."

"No, that's okay. I have some in the car. Max, while you're out there, bring in your journal to show Mr....Jerry." April waited for Max to leave before continuing. "It's a long story, but I'm afraid my daughter has some trust issues."

"She always seemed so animated on the phone and in her texts."

April looked toward the door. "You disappointed

her. She'll warm back up, but it may take some time."

Jerry wasn't sure what to say. "I didn't mean to disappoint her."

Max returned before April could answer. As she entered, Jerry noticed a marked difference in the girl's personality. He was about to mention it when Gunter appeared beside her. Jerry looked at April, whose brow was furrowed, showing she was obviously still in the dark about the transformation. Max handed her mother the water bottle and then giggled when she sat on the couch, and Gunter jumped up beside her, licking her face.

April took a drink of water and slid a glance to Jerry, who shrugged his shoulders. Jerry wanted to let her in on the joke but knew it was too early to mention Gunter, knowing he was at risk of either having April think him crazy or deciding he was trying to dupe them with some kind of scam. Jerry pointed to the notebook Max had brought in with her. "Is that the journal you've been keeping?"

Max handed it to him. "I wrote down everything just like you said."

Jerry opened the spiral journal and leafed through the pages detailing each dream. At the end of each writeup were starred bullets of things Max recalled about the dream. A smell, taste, or noise. On more than one page, Max mentioned hearing a bell. The notation nagged at him, as Patti had said she'd also heard a bell. Jerry used his finger to keep his place and looked at Max. "Tell me about the bell."

"What do you want to know?"

"What did it sound like?"

Max frowned. "I don't know, just a bell."

April turned toward her daughter. "I think what Jerry wants to know is was it a dinner bell, a doorbell, or deep like a church bell."

Gunter had calmed and was now lying with his head in Max's lap. Jerry watched as her fingers moved through the dog's fur. After a moment, her hands stilled. "Deep, like a church bell, only scarier."

Jerry nodded and continued to skim the pages, noting content Max hadn't shared with him before. No wonder, since it was ugly stuff. He flipped ahead to the final few pages, where Max wrote about the woman appearing outside of her dreams. The last page recalled the dream she'd had during the night and spoke of the woman grabbing her, and finding the bruises. Anger soared through his veins at the thought of anyone hurting the girl. He placed the journal on his lap and addressed April. "Have you read any of the journals?"

April shook her head. "No. Is something wrong?"

His gaze drifted to Max. "Did you tell your mother about the woman hurting you?"

Max lowered her eyes. When she spoke, her

words came out in a whisper. "No."

April's nostrils flared. "Hurt you? Who?"

Max blinked back tears. "The woman in my dreams."

April shook her head as if trying to comprehend what Max had said. "What do you mean the woman in your dreams hurt you? It was a dream. Dreams may scare you, but they can't hurt you."

Max brushed her hands through Gunter's fur once again.

April pointed at Max's hands. "What are you doing?"

Max looked to Jerry, and he blew out a sigh. "It's okay, Max. You can tell her."

"I'm petting Jerry's dog."

If ever a person looked like they wanted to run, it was April Buchanan. Jerry had to give her credit when she merely looked to him for an explanation. Jerry placed his hand on his chin, felt the two-day stubble, and realized he must look a fright. He thought about locking the door so she couldn't take Max and leave, but decided not to add kidnapping to his list of infractions committed since he'd left the force. "Mrs. Buchanan, there really isn't an easy way to lead into this conversation. Max can see ghosts."

April laughed. "She's told me. But we both know there are no such things as ghosts."

"There are spirits, and Max can see them." April

started to object, and Jerry held up a hand. "I see them too."

This time, her laugh was a nervous giggle. "Mr. McNeal, you don't expect me to believe there are ghosts floating around the room."

Jerry shook his head. "Some say they do, but in all my years, I've never actually seen one float. Some fade in and out, but from my experience, they walk. My Aunt Edna was in a wheelchair the last ten years of her life, and for two days during her visitation services, she stood beside her coffin greeting everyone who approached her coffin."

April sprang from the couch. "Max, I think it is time for us to go."

"But, Mom…"

"Don't but Mom me. I thought I was bringing someone here who could help you, not someone who…dammit, Max, listen to me!"

What April Buchanan didn't know was that Max couldn't move as she had a ninety-pound shepherd lying across her lap. April reached for Max's arm to help her along, and Gunter took her hand in his mouth. April's eyes grew wide, and she froze.

Max laughed. "I don't think he wants me to leave."

April gulped. "Wha…what is that?"

"It's my dog. Gunter, release."

Gunter let go of the hand but made no move to leave Max's lap.

April turned her hand back and forth, checking for marks. "There's nothing there."

Jerry held up his own arm to show the marks from his recent encounter with Gunter. "If he wanted to leave a mark, he would have."

Max's eyes bugged. "Whoa!"

April was less impressed. "He bit you?"

"Not on purpose. He was on the job, and I interfered."

April looked from Jerry to Max before reluctantly taking a seat in a recliner on the opposite side of the room. "What do you mean 'on the job'?"

Jerry could tell she was struggling but admired her willingness to at least try. "Gunter was a police dog in his prior life and thinks he is still on the job. He's helped me on numerous jobs since he found me."

"Found you?"

"I sure as heck didn't go looking for him." Gunter growled, and Jerry laughed. "He still gets a little miffed when I tease him about it."

April frowned. "You're saying he can understand you?"

"Seems to." Jerry thought about adding that they seemed to be able to communicate telepathically but didn't want to overload the woman's already fragile belief. "Anyway, we were working on a murder case in Tennessee, and Gunter found the body. Only the body was buried in the same grave as someone else, and I thought he was merely digging a hole. I tried to stop him when he was in the zone. It was my fault, but I learned my lesson."

April glanced in Max's direction. "Is that what happened when I tried to make Max get up?"

Jerry ran his hand over his head. "Perhaps he was trying to protect her, but I think it was more he knew I wasn't done talking to you both."

April looked toward the door. "You mean we can't leave until you say so?"

"No, ma'am. I assure you that you are free to leave anytime you wish. I won't stop you, nor will I allow Gunter to." Whether he actually had any control over the dog, Jerry did not know. He gave a nod to Max. "I hope you stay. If this spirit has taken to hurting Max, we need to find out what she wants."

April leaned forward in her chair. "Max, are you sure it wasn't just a dream?"

Jerry opened the journal to where Max spoke about the dream. He walked to where April sat and handed her the journal, pointing to the line where Max mentioned the bruise.

April read it and looked at Max. "Show me."

Max carefully pulled her collar back to display the bruise.

"Why didn't you tell me?"

Max met her mother's gaze. "Would you have believed me?"

April bit her bottom lip. "No."

"I'm not lying!"

April turned toward Jerry. "So what happens now? Do we need to call a priest or something?"

Jerry shook his head. "I don't think an exorcism will be necessary. We need to figure out who the spirit is and what she wants."

"She's not your friend. I asked her. She didn't tell me her name, but she got mad and said not all redheads are named Patti."

April scowled at Jerry. "So you purposely had my daughter interrogating a ghost."

"I asked her to ask the woman a question, yes." He directed his next comment to Max. "I'm sorry if that caused her to hurt you. I was just trying to make sense of why Patti knew about you and why she told me I needed to take your call."

April pulled herself straighter in her seat. "So back to my original question. What happens now?"

Jerry ran his hand over his head, searching for an answer. He couldn't talk to the spirit until she made contact. Unfortunately, he did not think that would happen if April were around. Spirits tended not to like to waste their time with non-believers. And while April was on the fence, the practical side of her brain still wasn't convinced. "Now, I'm going to have to ask you to make a difficult decision."

"I'm listening."

"I need you to let Max hang out with me alone."

"I will NOT allow my daughter to spend the

night with you."

Jerry held up his hand. "Nor am I asking you to. Tomorrow, in the light of day, Max and I will try to find the woman and see if we can figure out what she wants from us."

Max lit up. "Can I, Mom?"

April shook her head. "No."

Jerry blew out a sigh. "Mrs. Buchanan, I can't begin to put myself in your shoes. I know I'm asking a lot from you. But I wouldn't do it if I could figure out another way. I do not believe the spirit will show herself if you are with us. The fact that she hasn't shown up already proves my point. She has already hurt Max once. We have to presume she will do anything to get her point across."

"What kind of woman would hurt a child?"

"Her spirit is probably confused. My thinking is she latched on to Max because she knows she can see her." Jerry pivoted toward Max. "Did you feel anything when you came here today?"

"No. I was kind of mad, so I might have missed it."

"That's okay. You had a right to be upset. Are we good now?"

Max smiled and bobbed her head.

"April, I'm a man of honor. I will not harm your daughter. But you don't have to take my word for it. That dog over there is a police dog first and foremost. As such, he will not allow me or anyone else harm Max." Jerry held up his arm. "He did this when I tried to stop him from doing his job. Right now, his job is to protect Max."

"You're asking me to entrust my daughter to a man I don't know because she will be protected by a dog I cannot see."

Yes. "I'm asking you to allow me to help your daughter the only way I know how."

April nodded her agreement. "Okay. But know this, you harm one hair on her head, and no dog, living or dead, will be able to save you."

Max buried her face in Gunter's fur to hide her giggles, and Jerry nodded his understanding, then smiled and said, "Now that we have that out of the way, could I have the pleasure of taking you ladies to dinner?"

Chapter Eight

Freshly showered and clean-shaven, Jerry sat at the small kitchen table reading through Max's journal. He still had an hour before it was time to pick up Max and April for dinner, and he wanted to see if he could find any more similarities between the spirit visiting Max and what Patti had told him. That the two murders were connected was highly unlikely, but why else would Patti insist he take Max's call?

To Max's credit, each entry was legible and written in precise detail – as much as she could remember anyway. The visits started as dreams, with Max thinking the woman was about to be murdered. Halfway through, the entries showed that she knew the woman was already dead. The question remained, was the woman, in fact, alive when Max first picked up on her, or was that merely the way the vision appeared? Jerry took out his own notebook and jotted down that very question. In another entry, Max had thought the woman to be named Virginia. He skimmed through to see if there was any other mention and saw two, but neither confirmed. Max was not one to make a mistake. The name Virginia was no accident. While it might not be her name, he had to consider it a clue. Jerry made an asterisk and added the name to his notes.

Another thing that was mentioned on more than one occasion was the bells. Patti also mentioned hearing bells. Jerry noted that on his pad.

He continued reading and found a page where the visiting spirit had told Max in some detail what the man had done to her. Jerry read through the notes. *Jesus.* Patti had told Jerry the man had hurt her. However, she hadn't elaborated on the deed. Jerry made a note that simply read *raped and beaten.* That Max had to hear it was bad enough.

Jerry laid the pen on the table and placed his fingertips together in prayer style. Max's mother had said Max had trust issues. He'd also noted the look that passed between Max and her mother when Jerry had mentioned the domestic violence. April hadn't worn a wedding ring, nor were there any signs that she'd worn one recently. He tapped his index fingers against his lips, trying to get a lead on their situation. Nothing. *Their lives are not yours to fix, Jerry. You're here to help the spirit find her peace and nothing more.*

Jerry flipped to the next page of the journal and read Max's account about the previous night. *The woman came to me in my dream again. Only it didn't feel like a dream. She was angry because Jerry wasn't here. I told her he was coming, but that wasn't good enough. She wanted him here now. I was scared but didn't let her know. I told her Jerry wasn't a ghost, and I could not just make him appear. She didn't like my answer, so she grabbed me by the shoulder and pressed her fingers into it. It hurt. I yelled and told her so, and that's when my mom showed up. Mom told me it was just a dream. I told her it didn't feel like one, but she insisted it was. I slept with the light on the rest of the night. I can't wait for Jerry to get here. He will fix this. At least I hope so. I don't know what I will do if he doesn't. PS, Mom was wrong. It wasn't a dream. I have bruises on my shoulder! I'm not going to tell Mom. She will accuse me of getting into another fight. Only I haven't. Not lately anyway. I like my new school and have made some friends. I like Chloe the best. I can tell her everything. Almost everything, I haven't told her about Gunter because I promised Jerry I wouldn't. I didn't tell her about the bruises on the woman's neck and the reason she couldn't talk above a whisper.*

Jerry read the last line again and then added the bullets to his notes. He looked at his notes: *red hair, bells, Virginia, strangled*. He added "lighthouse" as he knew that was important and that the woman was wearing a sweatshirt with a lighthouse. Jerry flipped back to the notes he'd written in regard to Patti's case. Red hair, female, late twenties to early thirties. Bruises on the neck consistent with strangling. Rape, murder took place in the cemetery. Patti remembered hearing bells. *Consistent. Not so fast, McNeal. You're forgetting the murders took place seven hundred miles apart.*

Jerry rubbed his hand over the top of his head. *They're connected. I'd bet money on it.*

Jerry heard a noise and turned to see Gunter lying on the floor, panting. The dog had disappeared shortly after Max and her mother left.

"Yo, dog, this is getting ridiculous. You may be immortal, but she isn't." Jerry checked the clock and saw he still had some time until he needed to pick up Max. While he'd eaten breakfast, he hadn't had anything since. An inspection of the fridge found nothing but a few condiments. He checked the cabinets and didn't find anything to tide him over. "I'm going to the store. Wanna come?"

Gunter lifted his head, then lowered it back to the floor, his tongue hanging from his mouth as if he'd just walked ten miles. Jerry laughed. "Suit yourself. You know how to find me."

Jerry felt the pull the moment he got in the Durango. It let up the second he turned away from the lighthouse. He thought about turning around but knew there wasn't time, not if he found what he thought he'd find anyway. He saw the Mercantile and pulled to the curb. Crossing the road, he went inside. He was studying the colorful yard art when a woman greeted him.

"Can I help you find something?"

Jerry pulled a purple and green metal frog from the shelf. "I'll take this guy. I also need a cooler."

The woman took the frog from him and pointed. "We have a couple to choose from down that aisle."

Jerry found the cooler, and a man he knew had long left this world. Jerry stepped around the man and lifted a cooler from the shelf without a word. While he knew the man was a spirit, the energy surrounding the man appeared to be at ease. That was the thing about ghosts. Not all of them needed help. Some of them were just here to keep an eye on things, much like they had when alive. The cashier counter was in the middle of an aisle near the front of the store. As the woman started ringing him up, the gentleman spirit stood just behind her right shoulder, overseeing the sale. The woman looked over her shoulder once, but if she knew the spirit was standing there, she never mentioned it.

She pulled the tag from the frog and keyed in the number. "He's cute."

Jerry nodded his head in agreement. "My mom likes frogs."

The woman wrapped the frog in newspaper and placed him in a bag. "There are a few more over there if you decide he needs a friend."

The gentleman smiled. Jerry wondered if he approved of the attempt at an up-sale or the polite customer service. *Probably both.* "I'll keep that in mind."

The woman lifted the lid to the cooler and placed the frog inside, then motioned to the credit card machine to complete the sale.

Still doing good on time, Jerry headed to The Store, hoping it still was open. He needn't have worried, as the sign on the door said they were serving pizza until seven. If he hadn't already had dinner plans, he would have ordered one. The inside was small but clean with wide-spaced custom wood aisles that appeared well-stocked with necessities and staples to make simple meals. Unlike the Mercantile, the only spirits were on the shelves behind the long wooden counter that held the cash register. A statue of a chef stood just inside the door and reminded him of a photo his mother used to have hanging in her kitchen.

A tall man came out from the backroom and saw Jerry looking at the statue. "It was a gift when my mom purchased the store. He was missing a hand, so my mom fixed it."

Jerry looked closer. "Clever."

"We have cookies and pizza. We had bread pudding, but I'm afraid we're all out."

"Just my luck." Jerry had never had bread pudding before, but at the moment, everything sounded good. "I'll pass on the pizza for now, but I might have to take you up on those cookies."

The man grabbed some from the bakery case and

placed them on the counter while Jerry continued to shop. Jerry selected a loaf of bread and some chips and then went to the deli at the back of the store.

A woman came in from the back and wiped her hands on her apron. "What can I get for you?"

"Half a pound of ham and a few slices of American cheese."

The woman pulled the ham from the case. "I haven't seen you around. Are you new in town?"

Got to love a small town. "Staying at the campground for a couple of days."

The woman nodded. "We have daily specials if you get tired of cooking over a campfire."

"Good to know." Jerry walked around the store, picking up a few odds and ends, mostly because he was hungry and everything looked good.

The guy behind the counter went to the deli and grabbed Jerry's order from the woman, who Jerry came to find out was the man's mother. "Do you need anything else?"

Jerry placed the rest of his hoard on the counter. "A six-pack of Bud and some ice."

"Sure thing."

Jerry congratulated himself for making it out of the store without ordering a pizza. The kudos was short-lived when he plopped a cookie into his mouth while loading his bags in the car. He heard his grandmother chide him for spoiling his dinner and turned, half expecting to see her standing behind him. He was alone but knew her spirit was near. He removed the frog from the cooler and placed the lunch meat and cheese inside with the beer and ice. He thought about going back in to get some orange juice, checked the time, and decided against it. He'd disappointed Max once today. He wouldn't make that mistake again.

It took all of two minutes to reach Max and April's house. Max bolted out the door the moment he pulled into the driveway with April a few steps behind. April walked to the passenger side, and Max opened the back door.

"Where's Gunter?"

Jerry looked in the rear mirror. "Back at the camper."

"Why didn't you bring him?"

April looked over her shoulder. "Max, he probably didn't want to take the dog into the restaurant."

"But he's a ghost. It's not like anyone will see him."

Jerry nodded his head in agreement. "She's right. Gunter is usually with me everywhere I go. Only it seems he was a bit tuckered out."

April raised an eyebrow. "Ghosts get tired?"

Jerry glanced in the mirror and saw that Max was hanging on every word. "They do when they have a lady friend who's more than willing to keep them company living next door."

April cocked her head to the side. "Oh…oh. So you're saying Lady is in heat?"

"Appears that way."

"You mean Gunter can…?"

"Appears that way," Jerry repeated.

Max stuck her head between the seats. "Does that mean Lady is going to have puppies?"

Jerry looked over at April and then back at Max. "I guess time will tell. But I wouldn't mention it to Mr. Mills anytime soon. Something tells me he won't find it as amusing as the rest of us."

April clicked on her seatbelt. "What are you hungry for?"

"Food. I'm hungry."

April smiled a wide smile. "Do you like burgers?"

"Of course."

"Then you have got to try a Leroy Burger."

Jerry put the Durango into reverse. "The Port Hope Hotel it is."

Max gasped. "You know about the hotel?"

Jerry looked in the mirror and wiggled his eyebrows. "I had a feeling."

April laughed. "Or he read it on the sign when he was coming through town."

"Ha, busted!" Jerry backed out of the driveway and switched into drive. "I guess it would be pointless to ask for directions."

"Given we can practically see it from here, I'd

say so. Max, did you remember your seat belt?"

Jerry heard a click from the backseat.

"Yep."

"A little sooner next time, young lady."

"Yes, Mom."

Jerry's stomach rumbled as he pulled to the curb near the front of the brick building. He looked over at April and shrugged. "Didn't have lunch."

Several round picnic tables sat on the deck. Jerry followed as April and Max bypassed them, opting to sit inside. The way was blocked just inside the door. Once again, Jerry followed as the girls veered to the left. The inside of the building was furnished with simple square diner tables with arched metal back chairs. A long wooden bar sat toward the middle rear of the room, while a pool table took up most of the secondary room. The walls were equally painted blue and yellow/gold, showcasing the owner's penchant for Michigan football. What windows the room had were small and located near the ceiling, making it all but impossible to look out. While it solved the problem of not sitting with his back to the window, Jerry did prefer to have an escape route if a situation warranted it.

April stopped at an empty table near the wall by the air conditioner. "This okay with you?"

Jerry worked the tension from his shoulders. "Sure."

"Don't worry, Jerry. It's safe in here."

That Max had picked up on his thoughts didn't surprise him. She'd done it even before they'd met. Jerry looked about the room, noting a claw machine sitting beside a keno machine. To the left of the bar appeared to be a small office. He noted a door that led to the kitchen and another that possibly led to another way out of the building. With all exits covered, Jerry began to relax.

A waitress approached the table with a Bud Light, which she set in front of April, along with a lemonade for Max. She looked Jerry up and down, then smiled at April. "Girl, where've you been hiding this one?"

April blushed and looked at him as if seeing him for the first time. "Jerry's a friend of the family."

"I'm just messing with you, Lady. You deserve to have a little fun." The woman winked at Jerry. "Now, what can I get you, handsome?"

"A bottle of Bud."

"You got it. I know what these two want. Do you need a menu?"

Jerry shook his head. "I'll take a Leroy burger and fries."

"A single or double?"

The cookie hadn't even touched his appetite. "Better make it a double with the works."

Max giggled, and April bit her bottom lip.

Jerry looked from one to the other. "Did I miss something?"

"Nope!" both replied at the same time.

Chapter Nine

The moment he saw the waitress heading their way, Jerry knew he'd screwed up. The burger had two beef patties, each looking to be an inch thick. Though the patties looked uniform in their structure, he could tell they were not your run-of-the-mill preformed patties. Each patty had been hand-pressed in a ring, cooked to perfection, and now sat on a bun with lettuce, tomato, and onion, the whole of which was nearly as tall as the beer bottle sitting in front of him. The sandwich was accompanied by a full basket of crisp shoestring french fries.

Jerry eyed April's single burger, a sizeable offering in its own right, and Max's chicken tender basket, then lifted a fry and pointed it to each in turn. "The joke is on you, ladies, as I intend on eating every bite."

Max dipped a tender in barbecue sauce and took a bite. "Do you think you can?"

April dabbed her mouth with the napkin. "Max, don't talk with your mouth full."

"Oh, I'll finish it, but it won't be pretty. In fact, I may need a bib." Jerry turned the plate, trying to plan his attack, then pressed the whole thing with his hands. He lifted the beast and, after several attempts, finally managed a bite. He closed his eyes, enjoying the flavor, finished the bite, then started to take another and hesitated. "I'm going to be a while. Since you don't approve of talking while eating, maybe you should tell me about your town. Have you lived here all your life?"

Another look passed between April and Max. It was April who finally spoke. "We moved here two years ago after I divorced my husband."

That she hadn't referred to the man as Max's dad wasn't lost on Jerry. "Why Port Hope?"

"My friend Carrie lives here. We went to the same school just outside Detroit. She met a guy and moved here shortly after we graduated. I never pictured her as a farmer's wife, but he adores her, and she seems happy. They have a nice-size farm just outside of town. About the time I left Randy, Carrie's grandmother moved into a facility. Carrie was trying to figure out what to do with her house. The moment I told her what was going on, she insisted we come." April looked over at Max and smiled a grateful smile. "I don't know how we would have managed without her help. Carrie rents us the house for way less than she could get from anyone else. I found a job where I can work from home. It's not the most glamorous job, but it pays the bills."

Jerry took a sip of his beer. "What do you do?"

April's mouth was full, so Max answered for her. "Mom's a computer geek."

April shook her head. "I don't really work on them. I troubleshoot. When people call in, I have a list of things to have them try. If those things don't work, I arrange for them to have their computer looked at by a professional. As I said, not the most glamorous job."

Jerry thought of the laptop he'd purchased this morning and the fact that it was still in the box. "I'd think knowing your way around a computer would be a great asset. And at least you have a job."

Max took that opportunity to pounce on his comment. "You had a job. Why'd you quit?"

"Max, that is none of your business," April scolded.

"But I want to know. Jerry had the best job ever, and people believed him when he told them things. If I had a job like that and people believed me, I'd never quit. You had the perfect job. You were a police officer, Jerry. You got to help people, and you quit. I don't understand." Max was trembling, and it was clear his decision had been troubling her for some time.

Jerry set his burger down, wiped his hands on the napkin, and leaned back in his chair, choosing his words. "You're right. On the surface, it sounds like the perfect job. And for a long time, it was, because I'd finally found a job where I could use my abilities to help people. Lots of people, but then things changed, and I knew I wasn't going to be in control anymore. It wasn't an egotistical decision. I don't care about being my own boss or overseeing others, but this gift we have makes us different, and not everyone appreciates it for what it is. Maybe they are jealous, or it could be they simply don't understand it or believe in it.

"For the last six years, I've had a boss that understood my gift and allowed me to use it. I was able to follow my feelings and go where I was needed, but in doing so, some thought I was getting special treatment. I was, mind you, but that's not the point. I was hired to do the same job they were, and they thought I should be following the same rules. So, it was decided I needed to start adhering to a schedule, and well, I knew that meant I wouldn't be able to listen to my gut. Can you imagine knowing something was going to happen, and no one would listen to you?"

Once again, Max and April locked eyes.

Max was the first to break eye contact and turned her attention back to Jerry. "I don't understand. You said your boss believes you. Why would he change the rules if he believed you?"

"My boss did. He's the one that let me do my own thing for the last six years. But even bosses have bosses, and his boss didn't think what I was doing was fair to the other troopers."

Max sighed. "That sucks."

"Yeah, Max, it really does." Jerry picked up his burger and took another bite. He'd just finished the last of it when Max jerked her head up.

"I'm glad you don't have a job."

Jerry chuckled. "Is that a fact?"

"Yep. Because if you had a job, you'd be helping someone else instead of me."

April beamed at her daughter. "That's my girl. Always looking on the bright side."

Jerry nodded his agreement. "And now you understand why I had to make the choice that I did. Being a free agent allows me to go where the feeling takes me and help those most in need."

A frown flitted across April's face. She dug in her purse and pulled out a dollar, handing it to Max. "Why don't you give the claw machine a go."

Max grabbed the bill and hurried across the room.

April folded her hands on the table. "Mr. McNeal, when you told me you were coming, I was thrilled to know that Max would finally have someone she could talk to about all of this. I had no idea the woman in her dreams was real, nor that she'd been hurting my daughter. So your presence here really is a godsend."

Jerry ran his index finger over the rim of the beer bottle. "Why do I get the feeling there is a 'but' coming?"

She looked at him with nary a smile. "Because there is. I'm a single mother doing everything I can to keep a roof over our heads. It didn't dawn on me that I would have to pay you. If you can tell me what I owe you for driving all this way, I will see what I can do and make payments on the rest."

Jerry didn't even try to hide his confusion. "Mrs. Buchanan, I'm not sure what I said to set you on your heels, but I haven't asked for money, nor do I intend to. I'm here to help Max, not scam you."

"But you said you quit your job to become a free agent. You can't expect to do all of this without being paid. Gas, food, and lodging cost money. How will you manage?"

"Some people that know about my gift set up a bit of a trust fund that allows me to do this." *Okay, not the total truth but not a lie either*. "Between that and people such as yourself offering me lodging at no cost, I get by well enough."

April let out a relieved sigh. "You don't know what this means to us, Mr. McNeal."

Jerry watched as Max rounded the bar and went into the restroom. As she entered, he felt the hairs on the back of his neck tingle. "Call me Jerry, and I haven't done anything yet. Mrs. Buchanan, the bathrooms here, do they have a single stall or more than one?"

"It's April. And the bathrooms are as old as the building. I doubt you could fit more than one person in them."

Jerry drummed his fingers on the table. "Is Max capable of hurting herself?"

April frowned. "No, she never would. Why do you ask?"

Jerry wanted to tell the woman it was nothing, but it wouldn't be the truth. Something was wrong. He could feel it. "Go to the bathroom and knock on the door. Do it now!"

To April's credit, she left without another word, hurrying to the bathroom, knocking on the door, and calling Max's name.

Think, Jerry. GUNTER! Gunter, help Max!

April knocked once more, then went to the bar and demanded the key. Before she could reach the bathroom door, it opened, and Max hurried out with Gunter at her side. Her face was ghostly white, and she was trembling.

April put her arm around her and led her to the table, waiting until they were seated before questioning her. Gunter kept looking over his shoulder as if checking to see if they'd been followed.

April helped Max into the chair. The second Max sat, she burst into tears. April looked at Jerry, her brows knitted with concern.

Jerry leaned close to the girl. "Max, what happened in there?"

Max continued to sob.

The waitress came to the table. "Everything okay?"

April managed a smile. "Teenagers."

The woman nodded her head. "I get it. I was young once. Been a while, but the hormone trip was hell. I'll tell you that. Heads up there, Max. Things will get better."

The moment the woman walked away, Jerry leaned in again. "Come on, Max, talk to us."

Max looked up through tear-filled eyes. "I went to the bathroom. When I was done, I started washing my hands, and when I turned to dry them, the woman was there. Then she blocked the door and wouldn't let me out. I told her you were here, and she said I must bring you to her. Only, when I tried to leave, she wouldn't let me. She looked so mean, Jerry. Then Gunter showed up, and he was even meaner. He stood in between us, growling at her until she disappeared."

April pushed from the table and stormed to the bathroom. Jerry didn't expect the spirit to still be in there, but if she were, he'd put his money on the momma bear. April returned a moment later and focused her anger on Jerry. "This has got to stop."

"I understand."

April squared her shoulders. "No, you're not hearing me. I want it to stop tonight."

It doesn't work that way. Jerry lifted his hand to call the waitress over.

"What can I do for you, honey?"

"I'd like to pay the bill."

She smiled. "Oh, it's already been paid."

Jerry tilted his head. "Excuse me?"

The waitress bobbed her head. "Yep, see that man over there?"

Jerry looked to where she pointed and saw the officer that had responded to the scene earlier when he'd helped save the man's life. The office saw him looking and gave a little wave.

"Bill told me how you saved Hershel's life."

"I was in the right place at the right time."

"That's not what Bill said. Bill said that you were cool as a cucumber. The way you called it in and stayed at the scene until the ambulance took Hershel away."

"Jerry used to be a cop." Max sniffed.

"I knew there was something about you. I just couldn't put my finger on it. Anyway, your bill's paid." She gave a nod to April and Max. "All of it."

Jerry stood and walked over to Bill's table. Jerry hadn't noticed before, but standing here now, Bill reminded him a lot of Sergeant Seltzer, his old boss and longtime friend. Bill stood, and Jerry extended his hand, a mistake, as Bill had a killer grip, and the hand in question was still on the mend. He pulled his hand back the moment the man released it and swallowed the pain. "Thank you kindly for paying for our dinner."

"It was my pleasure."

Jerry looked over his shoulder. April and Max had left their table and were waiting near the door. He was glad to see Gunter standing next to Max. Jerry faced the man once more but kept his hand out of the man's reach. "Have a good night, sir."

"You too, son."

Jerry smiled.

"So, what do we do now?" April asked the moment they were in the Durango.

"We're going to have a talk with our friend." Jerry looked in the mirror. "Did she tell you where to find her?"

Max met his gaze. "She said you'll know."

Chapter Ten

The spirit was right in telling Max that Jerry knew where to find her. He'd felt her presence since heading up the lakeshore, a pull that was the strongest around the Pointe Aux Barques Lighthouse. He headed toward the campground, only instead of continuing to his camper, he stopped in the lighthouse parking lot and turned off the engine. "Do you want to wait in the camper or the Durango?"

April bristled. "I'd prefer to be near my daughter."

"We've already been through this. I don't think the ghost will show if you're with us."

"The ghost wants to talk to you. Why get Max involved?"

Jerry understood April's frustration, but the only way to get to the root of the situation was to meet it head-on. "Max is already involved."

"I don't like it."

"I wouldn't respect you if you did. Listen, I know the mom in you wants to protect your daughter, but take it from someone who knows. Max needs to learn how to protect herself."

April looked toward the lighthouse. "From what?"

Jerry brushed a hand over his head. "This ghost has attached herself to Max. Not like a possession, but she has singled out your daughter, and I need to make sure Max has the tools to handle this if it ever happens again."

April's bottom lip trembled. "And you can do that? Give her the tools?"

I haven't the slightest idea. "To be perfectly honest, I don't know."

Max, who'd been quiet to this point, leaned over the seat. "I've got to do this, Momma."

"But…"

"Don't worry. Gunter will be with me."

That seemed to ease April, as she nodded her consent.

Jerry opened his door, and Max followed suit, only instead of following him, she went to the passenger side and gave her mother a hug. A moment later, she joined him at his side.

Jerry knew they were headed in the right direction, as he felt the pull the moment they started toward the lighthouse. "Do you feel it?"

Max gulped. "Yes."

"Are you scared?"

"No. Are you?"

He knew she was lying but didn't call her on it. "I used to get scared, but I've gotten used to it now.

This is the pull – the feeling that lets you know you're heading in the right direction. Turn around and walk like you're going back."

She did as told, stopping after only a few feet. "It feels different."

He motioned for her to return and waited for her to reach him. "Remember this feeling. When you're going in the right direction, the energy feels good. When you aren't, it either stops or nags at you until you turn around."

"Neat."

"It can be – unless you're on the wrong path. Personally, I don't like it when the energy nags at me."

"I don't understand what you mean."

"You will. Your mind will be cluttered, and you won't be able to think straight." He laughed. "It might even feel like you're going crazy. If that happens, you'll need to clear your mind and consider the choices you've made recently or something you may have ignored. When you figure out what the energy wants, you'll be able to make a different choice, and you'll know when you're on the right path because it will feel as if a weight has been lifted from your shoulders."

"Have you felt it? The weight lifting?"

"I have. I had the clutter pretty bad before I left the state post, but as soon as I made the decision to leave, it was the most wonderful feeling in the world. It just felt right. Don't get me wrong, I was plenty scared, but I knew I'd made the right decision." Gunter growled. Jerry held his arm out, blocking her way. He pointed toward the northeast side of the lighthouse.

Max gasped. "It's her."

Jerry knelt in front of Max, keeping his voice to a whisper. "Let me do the talking. If she gets angry, stay calm. Stay with Gunter. She's afraid of him, so you'll be safe."

Max nodded her agreement, and they continued.

She was sitting under a tree, with her legs curled under her, throwing tiny pebbles towards the water below, oblivious to their approach. Though she had red hair and a slim figure and looked remarkably similar to his friend Patti, he knew the woman sitting in front of him was not her – the woman's energy was much darker than that of his friend. Whereas Patti was unsure of what happened to her, he felt the spirit in front of him remembered. And that knowledge fueled her rage.

Gunter growled, and she looked in their direction, focused on Max, and narrowed her eyes.

Jerry stepped forward, deliberately moving in front of Max to draw the spirit's attention. He waved his hand toward Max. "From here on out, this girl is off limits. You deal with me and only me."

The woman tossed the remaining pebbles toward the water, wiped her hands on her pants, and looked at Max. "I thought you said he was good. He doesn't have a clue."

Jerry firmed his voice. "I said you deal with me."

"I'm dead. I don't follow the rules. If you were as good as she said, you would already know that." To prove her point, she disappeared and reappeared directly in front of Max.

Gunter moved between them and growled a vicious warning.

The spirit took a step back. "Who are you that you can control the dead?"

"The dog is here of his own free will. I don't control him."

"I don't believe you! It's some kind of trickery. You didn't come to help. You came to capture my soul the same way you captured his. You say you want to help, but I felt you here earlier today. You should have let me know when you arrived, yet you did nothing. I was here, and you knew it."

Way to go, McNeal; you've been here less than seven hours, and you've already pissed off both Max and the spirit. You have a way with the ladies. No wonder you're still single. Jerry shook off the guilt. "You're right. I did feel you."

"Then why did you not come?"

"Because I was waiting for Max."

"Again with the lies."

"I wanted to wait for Max before I came to see you. I was also tired from the long drive, so I closed my eyes. I slept longer than I expected." He nodded toward Max. "I let you both down, and for that, I am sorry."

The spirit ignored his apology. "More lies. She came, and yet you left, so I had to find you!"

No, you found Max and scared the crap out of her. Don't go there, McNeal. It won't help the situation. "I needed to talk to Max first to see what she knew."

The woman narrowed her eyes and pointed a finger at him. "So that you could trap my soul."

So I could what?! Jerry struggled to stay calm. "I don't know who's filled your head with that crap, but I assure you people are not capable of trapping souls."

"They are too. I saw it in a movie."

There were no televisions on the other side, at least he didn't think there were, so she had to be speaking of one she'd seen while alive. "What movie?"

"*Ghostbusters.*"

It was Max who'd said it, but the woman nodded her agreement. Jerry shot Max a look, and the girl shrugged her apologies and clamped her hand over her mouth.

"I've seen spirits for as long as I can remember, and never once have I been even remotely inclined to capture their soul. And I assure you both," he gave them each a long look, "that I couldn't even if I wanted to. No one can. What I can do is help you find some peace if you will let me. But that will come with conditions."

"I knew it was a trick."

Jerry sighed a heavy sigh. "No trickery. I just want your promise."

The ghostly spirit stared at him. "What kind of promise?"

"That you will leave Max alone from this moment and even after I'm gone. You are not to invade her dreams. You will not harass her, and you will never lay another hand on her."

She laughed a haunting laugh. "And you'll take me at my word?"

Jerry nodded. "I will."

A sly smile crossed her lips. "And if I break my promise?"

Jerry hadn't a clue how to respond until Gunter growled, and he knew that was the leverage he needed. "I believe you just received your answer."

The spirit faded in and out several times before disappearing altogether.

Max stepped up beside him. "Where'd she go?"

I have no idea. "I think she's weighing her options."

"Do you think you made her mad?"

Probably. "I think she's scared, and being a bully is the only way she can feel like she's in control."

"If ghosts can't get hurt, then why are they

scared?"

"As a rule, spirits are free to move about from place to place. But sometimes, they become confused and stay earthbound. It may be they're afraid of leaving their loved ones or that perhaps something happened that they can't make sense of, which holds them here. My friend Patti was murdered, and the trauma of what happened caused her spirit to linger. Once she recalled what happened and we found her body, it helped her to recall what happened to her and helped bring her and her family closure. If we can figure out what happened to this woman, we might be able to help her find peace. I think we're done for the night. Let's head back to your mom. I'm sure she's worried." Jerry swatted a mosquito as Max fell in beside him. Relief washed over him when Gunter moved to his side. Gunter would have stayed next to Max if the woman's spirit was still near.

"Did you find her?" April asked the moment they reached the Durango.

Max climbed into the backseat, and Gunter jumped in beside her. "Yeah, you should have heard Jerry. He told her a thing or two."

Jerry fastened his seatbelt and started the Durango. "I just asked her to leave Max alone."

April raised an eyebrow. "What did she say?"

Max leaned up between the seats. "Nothing. She disappeared."

April looked over her shoulder. "Sit back and put your seatbelt on. Jerry, does that mean it's over?"

"No. But I don't think she'll be bothering Max again."

"Are you sure?"

No. "Fairly sure. The woman knows Gunter protects Max. She's afraid of him, so she'll back off, at least for now. I'll try to contact her again tomorrow and see if we can figure out what's troubling her."

"And I get to skip school!"

"I like to think of it as an educational field trip." Jerry glanced in the mirror and winked at Max. "Only you won't be turning in a research paper."

"Apparently, you're the talk of the town."

Jerry glanced at April. "How so?"

"Carrie called while I was waiting for you. She'd heard about you saving Hershel's life." She laughed. "One of the perks of living in a small town."

"It didn't happen in your town."

April laughed. "Close enough. You hang around, they may even give you the key to the city."

Jerry glanced in her direction once more. "You're kidding, right?"

April smiled. "Hang around long enough, and they may even throw you a parade."

Jerry couldn't tell if she was being serious or not, but he didn't plan on sticking around long enough to find out.

"Is that a cop thing?"

"Is what a cop thing?" Jerry asked, not taking his eyes off the road.

"Driving with both hands on the wheel." She mimicked his position. "Hands at ten and two just like the instructor says."

"Not hardly. If I were in my cruiser, I would be doing the cop lean."

She laughed. "What's that?"

"Driving with my left hand and checking my computer with my other."

"They have computers in the cop cars? Fancy. So the ten and two are for our benefit?"

"I'm keeping both hands on the wheel because I've seen the size of the deer in this state."

"We do have more than our share."

"The waitress at Denny's said she'd hit three in three years."

"Max's teacher hit one the day she bought her car."

"Yeah, she was not very happy about it either."

Jerry looked in the mirror at Max. "I can't say as I blame her."

"There's one!"

Jerry pressed on the brake but continued after seeing the deer grazing well off the side of the road. "You have a beautiful state, but I could do without the deer."

"I don't mind the deer so much, but I could do

without the mosquitoes."

"I may have had a couple of those find me at the lighthouse."

"Me too," Max chimed in.

"Be sure to use some tea tree oil on them when we get home, so they don't swell. Mosquitoes tend to like Max," April told him as he pulled into their driveway. "Thank you again for coming, Mr.... I mean Jerry. I do wish there was a way I could pay you."

"Actually, there is."

April paused with her hand on the door handle. "Yes?"

"I was wondering if I could borrow your Internet tomorrow. I bought a new computer, and I was hoping to get it set up."

April's shoulders relaxed. "You should be able to use the hotspot on your phone. Wi-fi can be tricky around the lakeshore. Just in case, I'll lend you my hotspot."

"You don't need it?"

"Only if the cable goes out. That happens, and I know where to find you. Max, run in and grab it, will you? It's in the top drawer of my desk."

"Okay." Max opened the door and jumped out, with Gunter following close behind.

"Are you sure she's safe?"

"I don't think there will be a problem tonight. Tomorrow, I will figure out how to reach the woman."

"Just to be safe, I think I'll have Max sleep with me tonight."

The front door opened, and Max and Gunter came running out. Jerry was grateful for the interruption.

***

Jerry sat at the kitchen table, drinking a beer and playing with his cell phone while waiting for his computer to finish installing the updates. He'd already checked his e-mail via his phone but wanted to have his computer ready just in case. He skimmed through Facebook, stalking his parents and smiling at a new photo his mom had posted of her sitting in her pink golf cart. Nearly the color of Pepto-Bismol, it suited her just fine. She beamed as she stared into the camera, and he wondered if the smile was just for the lens or because of something his dad had said.

Thinking of the camera made him think of Holly. He wondered if she really had a mind to contact him. Then again, she wouldn't have reached out to Seltzer if she hadn't. *So why haven't I heard from her? Probably because she's busy.* Jerry clicked on the Facebook search, typed in the name Holly Wood, and scrolled down until he found the right profile. He knew it was her, as he'd seen that picture before. It was a photo of Gunter, his face slightly covered with freshly fallen snow taken the night they had rescued her. The photo was in a heart-shaped frame with the words "My Hero." It was one of two photos Jerry knew to have been taken after the K-9's death. Jerry wondered what she would think if she knew her life had been saved by a ghost. He clicked on her profile, but she had her page locked down, limiting what could be seen by random strangers who might try stalking her page. *Smart Lady.* Jerry's finger hovered over the "add friend" icon as he had done so many times before, and just as he'd done in the past, he backed out of his account without pressing send. While he had the ability to see when bad things would happen, that gift did not include the power to see his future. When it came to his personal life, Jerry McNeal was as vulnerable as everyone else.

Chapter Eleven

The breeze filtering in from Lake Huron was crisp and strong enough to send the curtains flittering to the ceiling. Seagulls screeched overhead, and in the distance, a dog barked. Gunter growled a low warning. Jerry checked the clock to find it was just after four and placed a hand on the shepherd to silence him. He'd told Max to call him when she was up and about but didn't expect to hear from her anytime soon. He went to the counter and pulled a toaster pastry from the box, unwrapped it, and stuck it in the toaster before heading to the bathroom.

The pastry was waiting for him when he returned. He peeked out the side window, and the sky was just beginning to show the first glimpse of morning sun. He left the pastry in the toaster, dressed in shorts, then pulled on his running shoes.

The sight of the sneakers had Gunter spinning in circles. Jerry smiled. "I guess I'm not the only one who misses our runs."

Gunter jumped up, placing his paws on Jerry's chest. Jerry scratched the K-9 behind the ears before motioning him down. They walked on the lane heading toward the lighthouse. Jerry expected to feel the pull and was mildly surprised when it didn't come. He paused, using the bench of a picnic table to do some leg stretches while Gunter sniffed around the base of a tree. The dog sprinted to his side when Jerry started jogging toward the main road. "Go easy on me, fellow. It's been a while."

The duo made their way toward M25, then headed south toward Port Hope, watching as the sky to his left filled with brilliant pink, orange, and yellows hues. He saw movement to his right as a deer bolted, its whitetail all that remained visible as it sprang across the field. As Jerry continued, he spied a flock of birds wandering in the open field. At first glimpse, he thought they were buzzards or vultures, but as he drew closer, he realized they were a flock of wild turkeys. The tom must have sensed their presence, as he puffed up and ushered his group further into the field. A car approached. The driver honked and raised his hand as he passed. Jerry made a lazy loop and headed back the way he came. By the time he reached the lighthouse, the sun shone as a massive orange ball just breaching the water. He spent several moments stretching, then sat on top of the picnic table watching the sunrise and taking photos with his cell phone. Jerry had borne witness to some amazing sunrises in his lifetime and never grew tired of this simple pleasure. Overcome with the sheer beauty of the sun lifting over the lake and unable to capture the essence of it to his satisfaction, Jerry pocketed his phone and simply watched until the ball lost its glow and became too intense to view.

A dog barked, and Gunter answered with one nearly identical. He took a few steps toward the campground, then hesitated, trotting back to Jerry and sitting on his haunches as he looked longingly toward the campsite and whined.

Jerry laughed. "You might as well go. Any harm has already been done."

Gunter barked an eager bark, took a step, and promptly disappeared.

Jerry was still staring in the direction where he'd last seen the K-9 when he saw movement in a nearby tree. He watched the black shadow wind downwards, coiling around the tree as if a giant caterpillar had come to life, slowly making its way to the earth below. Once on the ground, the shadow parted, becoming eight jet-black baby squirrels moving forward in cautious leaps and bounds. A car drove past, sending all eight squirrels scampering back up the tree, only to repeat the initial process once the threat was gone. Fascinated by both their color and movement, he remained still, watching to see if they would make it to their destination. On three separate occasions, a vehicle drove past, and each time, the octet would retreat to their tree of birth, clutching the bark, tails flickering as they anxiously waited for the danger to pass. Jerry continued to watch, marveling at their unity. Not once did a single squirrel decide to move on without the others. Not once did a frightened sibling retreat on its own. They were a family unit acting as a single entity.

As they gathered their courage and crossed the yard, Jerry saw them as a hardened Marine unit making its way across enemy territory. On occasion, the procession would stop, each sticking its head up, surveying its surroundings. Nothing sighted, they lowered, took four leaps, then repeated the process. It took them nearly twenty minutes to leave their nest and cross forty feet of open ground, not because they were dallying but because they were on a recon mission. A successful one at that, because they made it to the rally point where they converged with others rejoicing in carefree play in a thick pine tree closer to the building. Filled with pine needles, the tree proved to be a safe zone, where the babies were shielded under the protection of nature's camo.

Jerry heard someone clear their throat. He turned to see a man standing on the porch of the caretaker's house, which had a sign that said no trespassing. The man wore black pants and a billowy white shirt, neither of which appeared to be from this century. The gentleman saw Jerry looking and strolled in his direction. He held a pipe between his teeth. As he approached Jerry, he removed the pipe and extended his hand.

"The name's Peter. I haven't seen you around here before."

Though Jerry knew he was a spirit, the man had a strong presence and firm grip. The moment he released his hold on Jerry's sore hand, Jerry was able to speak. "Just arrived yesterday. I'm here to help a lady you may have seen around. She stays around the lighthouse and seems a bit lost."

The man puffed on the pipe. "Lost, you say? You must mean the redhead. A real looker, that one. But a sorry soul if I've ever seen one. I hope you can help her."

"How about you? Is there anything I can do for you?"

"Me? No, I'm where I'm supposed to be. The sea tried to take me away, but I've returned to finish my job. Just heading to the light to see my wife. She helps out when I'm not about. I best be spelling her now. You take good care now, will you?"

"Yes, sir, I will."

Peter left without another word, walking to the base of the lighthouse. He stopped, raised his hand as if in greeting, then was gone.

Jerry was so focused on the lighthouse that he nearly missed the tingle that rose up the back of his neck, a warning that the spirit of the redhead was near. He scanned the perimeter and saw her standing near the lake side of the lighthouse, staring at him as if she'd been watching him the whole time. *Way to go, McNeal. You let your guard down again.* He pulled out his phone and dialed April's number.

"Hello?"

"It's Jerry. I know I am supposed to pick up Max…"

She cut him off. "You're not going to disappoint her again, are you?"

"I'm not trying to, or you either, for that matter. I am wondering if you can bring her to me."

"When?"

"Now. I'm at the lighthouse. The spirit is here. I don't need Max to do what I need to do, but as I've mentioned before, I think her being here will help her deal with this in the future."

"We'll be right there. Do you want me to stay or drop her off?"

"It's up to you, but I don't know how long it will take. Tell Max to approach slowly and use her intuition to join in if she feels the need."

"Okay, I'll drop her off but will have my cell with me."

Though her words said otherwise, Jerry could hear the trepidation in her voice. "Don't worry, April. I'll look after her."

Jerry ended the call, pocketing the phone as he started toward the spirit, walking in slow, deliberate steps to give Max time to join them. As he neared, her energy felt somewhat lighter, and he sensed a vulnerability in her he hadn't felt the evening prior.

Her bottom lip quivered, and he wondered at the transformation. The entity standing before him was not an angry spirit but a tortured soul. She made no move to run away. Not that she needed to run; she was a spirit. If she wanted to leave, she would only have to disappear. Another change was the fingerprint bruising that stained her otherwise milky white neck, a pattern that mimicked the bruising on Patti's neck and one he hadn't noticed the evening prior. Unusual, as it had been light enough that he should have been able to see the marks.

She saw him staring. Her hand went to her throat as she faded in and out.

Jerry stopped and stood open-palmed. "Please don't go. I'm here to help."

"Where's the girl?" When she spoke, her words were barely above a whisper.

"On her way."

"I didn't mean to hurt her."

"But you did." His words were not meant to upset the spirit but to show he was the one in charge and that inappropriate behavior would not be tolerated, especially by a ghost who chose not to follow the rules.

"I'm sorry."

Jerry chose to ignore the apology. The last thing he wanted was to give her an easy out she could use anytime she did something that wasn't acceptable. "If I'm going to help you, I will need to ask you

some questions. Some of them might be difficult.
Let's start with your name?"

"Ashley…Ashley Marie Fabel."

"My name is Jerry McNeal. What's your
birthday?"

"January 22, 1991. The girl said you're a cop."

"I was."

Her brows knitted together. "I thought you could
help."

"I can."

"But you're not a cop anymore."

"I still have connections."

She faded in and out several times.

"Stay with me, Ashley. I drove a long way to get
here and wouldn't have done that if I didn't think I
could help."

Jerry heard a car door slam and knew without
looking that Max had arrived. She did as directed
and approached slowly. He hoped she didn't make
mention of the fact that Gunter was nowhere in sight.
"Max, good of you to join us. This is Ashley Fabel.
I was just in the process of asking her some
questions. You can ask questions if I miss anything."

Max scratched at a bug bite on her leg. "Okay."

"Ashley, are you from this area?"

She shook her head. "No. I was just visiting."

"You were here to see the lighthouse," Max
offered.

"Yes, it was my dream to visit every lighthouse

before I died." Ashley sighed. "It didn't happen. Do you know if my family knows I'm dead?"

Jerry exchanged glances with Max, who shook her head. Jerry nodded to Max. "You seem to have a read on this. Go ahead."

"I think they know you are missing, but they don't know where to look for you." Max looked at Ashley. "Did you not tell them where you were going?"

"To a point. I told them I was going for a drive." She shrugged. "I'd done it in the past. Just start driving with no destination in mind. My family is fairly overprotective, and I'd just feel smothered at times."

Jerry rocked back on his heels. "Was there a reason for them to be overprotective?"

She shrugged her shoulders. "I didn't think so, but look where that got me."

Jerry felt she was holding something back, but she didn't seem to want to talk about it. "Where are you from, Ashley?"

She hesitated for a moment. "Boston."

Max sighed.

Jerry knew the reason for Max's disappointment. "Max picked up on Virginia, only she thought it was your name."

"Do you have any connection to Virginia?"

"No, not that I know of."

"Do you know the person who murdered you?"

"He said his name was John Smith."

Jerry chided himself for not having remembered his notebook, not that it mattered, since the name was probably an alias. "You said he told you his name, so you didn't actually know the man?"

"No, I met him in Port Huron."

"So, what, you met, and you two decided to go sightseeing together?"

Ashley narrowed her eyes. "You think I was promiscuous just because I traveled on my own? What about you? I don't see a ring on your finger. Is that because you're a man whore?"

Jerry chuckled. "I deserved that. I'm sorry, the cop in me tends to jump to conclusions. Allow me to rephrase: you said you met the man in Port Huron. Where did you meet and how did you end up here together?"

"I'd planned on traveling through Michigan and wanted to see every lighthouse in the state. I started in Detroit at the Bar Point Shoal Light station and had seen and photographed eleven lighthouses by the time I reached Fort Gratiot. The Fort Gratiot Lighthouse is part of the Coast Guard Station, and I wouldn't have been able to get a good shot of the lighthouse, so I decided to park at Lighthouse Park and walk up the beach a little way to get my pictures. I'd just finished taking them when I saw John."

A couple holding hands was walking in their direction. Jerry realized that, to the naked eye, it would look as if he and Max were alone near the bushes behind the lighthouse. "Do you ladies mind if we move to the picnic tables? I don't want anyone to get the wrong idea."

A look of regret crossed Ashley's face, and she began walking toward the tables without comment. Max grabbed Jerry's arm as he started to follow. "Why is she being so nice?"

"Maybe we got through to her last night."

"Where's Gunter?"

Jerry felt his cheeks turn red. "Visiting Lady."

"Oh." Max giggled as they both hurried to the table. She sat beside Jerry, who resumed the questions the moment they were seated.

"So you saw this John guy, and what, you just started talking to him?"

"Yes. I didn't see the harm."

Jerry held up his hand. "Wait, did you initiate contact, or did he?"

Ashley closed her eyes briefly, then opened them again. "He did. The sun was pretty bright, and he made a quip about how I should put on a hat, so I didn't burn."

"And you said?"

"Nothing. I was done taking photos when I saw him, so I headed back to my car."

Max pulled her phone from her pocket and began texting someone.

Jerry continued with the questions. "Did he

follow you?"

"No, I didn't think so at the time. He was still on the beach taking pictures when I left."

"And you drove straight up the coast?"

"Yes. No… I stopped at Panera to get a sandwich."

Max looked up from her phone. "Did you eat inside or use the drive-thru?"

"I went inside because I had to go to the bathroom, but I was in a hurry to see as many lighthouses as I could before stopping for the night, so I ordered my food to go."

Max tapped the keys on her phone, and Jerry realized she wasn't texting. She was taking notes. *Way to go, McNeal, outsmarted by a twelve-year-old.* "Did you make any more stops between Panera and Port Sanilac?"

Ashley raised an eyebrow. "Are you a lighthouse man?"

Jerry shook his head. "No, but I felt your presence there when I drove up yesterday morning. Did you make any more stops?"

"No…wait, yes, I did. I wasn't sure what to expect as I drove north and was about to turn around to get gas when I saw a big gas station on the right."

Max looked up from her phone. "The one with the big flag?"

Ashley nodded. "That's the one. I don't remember the name."

"It's enough. Then what?"

"Then I drove to Port Sanilac and took photos of the lighthouse. I may have hopped the fence and taken a selfie leaning against the base. I remember hoping I didn't get arrested. Looking back, it would have been better if I had."

"But you didn't see this John guy there?"

She shook her head. "Nope. Not in Harbor Beach either. I didn't see him again until I got to Pointe Aux Barques. He beat me there."

"And you didn't find it strange that he was there?"

She laughed. "I've had a long time to Monday morning quarterback things, Mr. McNeal. Hindsight and all, yes, it was strange. Like how did he know where I was going when I didn't tell him? At the time, I just thought he was doing the same thing I was doing. Taking photos of lighthouses."

Jerry ran his hand over his head. "You said you've had time to rehash everything. Did you ever come up with an answer about how he knew where you were going?"

"I did. The first time I saw John was on the beach in Port Huron. It is not a normal beach, more like crushed-up pebbles or something. Anyway, I'd stopped to kick some of the stuff out of my shoe, and when I bent over, my lighthouse map blew away."

"And he picked it up?"

"No, I did. Then I laughed and made a comment

about not being able to find the next lighthouse without my map."

The couple that had passed earlier walked closer. As they did, the woman smiled at Max. "A nice day to skip school and hang out with your dad, isn't it?"

"He's not my dad. We're just hanging out."

As soon as the words left her mouth, Jerry knew he was in trouble.

The woman grabbed hold of the gentleman's arm, dragging him to the next table, where she pulled out her cell phone and made a call.

"Max, do me a favor. Text your mom and tell her to come up here right away."

Max looked at Ashley and frowned. "But you said Ashley won't talk to you if Mom's here."

Jerry nodded to the couple. "Ashley will have to wait until after I convince the police I'm not a pedophile."

Chapter Twelve

Jerry had just finished texting Seltzer to give him a heads-up when April sped into the parking lot, kicking up gravel as the car skidded to a stop. She'd barely shut off the engine before jumping out and running to where Max and Jerry were sitting. April grabbed her daughter's cheeks with both hands and turned her head from side to side. "What's wrong? Did she hurt you?"

Jerry chuckled. "Just what did she tell you?"

"Only that I had to come right now."

Max's eyes went wide. "That's what you told me to say!"

"So you're okay?"

"Yeah."

"Maxine Buchanan, don't you ever do that again. You nearly gave me a heart attack."

The woman who'd made the call walked up to the table with her cell phone pressed to her ear. "Are you the girl's mother?"

"I am."

"The dispatcher wants to talk to you."

April looked to Jerry. "What dispatcher?"

"The police. The lady thinks Jerry is a perv,"

Max offered.

The woman became defensive. "They were standing by the bushes until he saw us coming, and then he moved her to the picnic table where she sat right beside him. What was I supposed to think?"

Jerry pointed toward the phone. "Maybe you should just talk to the lady."

April pressed the phone to her ear and walked to the front of her car. Though Jerry tried, he couldn't hear a word of what was said. She motioned Max over and handed her the phone. Max came back, asked him his birth date, and left once more. After about ten minutes, they both returned. April handed the phone to the woman.

The woman listened for a couple of minutes, bobbing her head up and down as she stared at Jerry. Finally, she hung up the phone and slipped it into the cargo pocket of her capris. "I'm sorry, I didn't know you were a police officer."

Jerry wanted to tell the woman she shouldn't have been meddling, but the truth of the matter was the world needed more people like her – especially when it came to looking out for kids. He smiled a sincere smile. "You didn't do anything wrong."

"I just didn't want to see anything happen to the child."

"I know."

The woman went over to her husband, who'd remained neutral during the whole ordeal, and they left hand in hand.

"You're not mad at her?" Max asked as soon as the couple was out of earshot.

Jerry leveled a look at her. "What if I had kidnapped you? That woman could have saved your life. Maybe if someone had looked after Ashley, her outcome would have been different."

"Ashley?"

"That's the name of the ghost, Mom. You should've been here. Jerry sounded like a real cop."

April smiled. "The dispatcher seems to think Jerry is a real cop. A Pennsylvania State Trooper, to be exact. I thought you said you quit?"

"I did. Seltzer is covering my ass." He looked at Max. "Sorry for the language."

"Do you think she'll come back?"

"No, she knows I'm a cop."

"Not the lady, Ashley."

"I hope so. I still have some questions for her."

April sighed. "You two do what you're doing, and I'll wait in the car."

Jerry pulled the key to the camper from his pocket. "The camper would probably be more comfortable."

To Jerry's surprise, Ashley reappeared the moment they were alone. Sitting in the same spot she'd been before, she crossed her arms and jutted her chin in his direction. "You must have been telling the truth when you said you have connections."

"I do." Jerry sat facing her and motioned for Max to do the same. "So you said he didn't raise any red flags?"

"He wasn't a creep or anything, and he seemed to know a lot about the history of the lighthouse. Heck, for all I know, it's because he googled it on the drive up. Anyway, we talked, and the guy was charming." She grew quiet.

After a few moments, Jerry pushed for more. "How charming?"

"Charming enough for me to agree to hang around town for the rest of the day. We sat on the stoop to the caretaker's porch and talked. Mostly, I did the talking. I guess I enjoyed talking to someone who wasn't family. He asked, and I divulged all. I was even foolish enough to tell him I'd left without telling my family where I'd gone." Her eyes darted to Max. "I'm dead because I'm stupid. You let this be a lesson to you. You want to hear the real zinger, the jerk was driving a van with a bed in the back, and I got in of my own free will."

The hairs on the back of Jerry's neck started to crawl. Patti's killer was also driving a van. *It is just a coincidence, McNeal.* "Do you remember anything else about the van?"

She laughed. "It was one of those windowless panel vans that the police warn you to stay away from."

"What did Mr. Smith look like?"

"White. Around six foot with brown hair."

"That's not much to go on, Ashley. Did he have any distinguishing features? Any piercings, a tattoo maybe?"

Tears welled in her eyes, and she started to fade.

"What is it, Ashley? Do you remember something?"

"Hash marks."

Jerry held her gaze. "What do you mean hash marks?"

"On his chest. Like when you are keeping count of something. He pulled back his shirt and showed me, telling me they were his conquests. He touched my face and told me he'd soon have one for me. I laughed and jerked away, as I knew I wasn't sleeping with the guy. That's when he punched me right in the jaw. I didn't see it coming. When I woke up, it was dark, and I was in the back of the van. I tried to move, but my wrists and feet were tied. I had a cloth in my mouth so I couldn't scream. It was quiet. He took off his shirt, heated a pocketknife with a lighter, then used the knife to make another cut." She faded then returned. "I don't want to do this anymore."

Jerry placed his hand on hers. "We don't have to talk about that. How many hash marks? Do you remember?"

"Eight, I think. I only got a glimpse before he

sucker-punched me."

"Do you know where your body is buried?"

"No. Only that it was dark, but around here, that could be any field."

Or cemetery. "Do you remember the date?"

"August 16. I remember because they were doing Elvis tributes on the radio."

Jerry looked at Max. "Do you have any questions?"

"Where's your car?"

She nodded toward the parking lot. "Parked right over there when I last saw it. It was a rental."

"Were there any bells?"

Ashley's hand traced the bruises on her throat, and then she was gone.

"I'm sorry, Jerry, I didn't mean to upset her. I wish she would have answered about the bells."

"Max, not all answers are given with words." Jerry touched his throat to further his meaning.

***

Jerry sent Max home with April, promising to pick her up after he made a few calls. Freshly showered, he sat in the recliner and dialed Seltzer's number.

"Since you're calling from your cell, I take it you're not calling for bail money."

"Nope. Thanks for saving my ass once again."

"Care to fill me in?"

"Woman sees man alone with young girl, finds

out the said man is not the girl's father and calls police. End of story."

"Too bad we don't get more of those calls."

"My sentiments exactly. Hey, remember why I'm here?"

"The 'could be something could be nothing' case?"

"That's the one. I think it's a something."

"I'm listening."

"Aside from both victims looking nearly identical, they were both brutalized, raped, and eventually strangled in a white van, at night."

"Sounds like it has teeth, aside from the fact they were 700 miles apart. Any leads on the suspect?"

"John Smith. White male, around six foot tall with brown hair."

"Doubtful it's his real name. Even if it was, do you know how many John Smiths there are?"

"One or two. The victim's name is Ashley Marie Fabel. Date of birth January 22, 1991, five foot six with red hair and green eyes. I suspect her family knows she is missing but don't know she's dead. Tread lightly; Miss Fabel said she's from Boston and made mention of her family being connected."

"To what?"

"That's for us to find out."

"I'll do some digging. Anything else?"

"Yeah, we're dealing with a real psycho. Ashley said the guy keeps track of his victims by cutting

what she referred to as hash marks into his chest.
Said he heated the knife with a lighter before slicing
it into his skin. She watched him make the mark for
her the night he killed her."

"Am I going to regret asking how many marks
she saw?"

"She wasn't sure but thinks she counted eight."

"Including hers or before?"

"Not sure."

"Have you notified authorities?"

"No body, no crime."

"You got a plan?"

Jerry laughed. "Do I ever?"

"No, but that's never stopped you in the past.
You'll get 'er done. In the meantime, I'll shake some
trees of my own. I'll let you know what falls out."

Jerry had no sooner ended the call than it rang
again. He looked to see Savannah's name on the
screen. "I was just fixing to call you. Are you
reading my mind again?"

"No, I was calling to thank you!"

"What did I do?"

"Very funny. The bathroom looks amazing! I
can't believe you did all of that in the short time you
were there. How much do we owe you?"

Caught up on things here, Jerry had completely
forgotten about the renovations he'd made to the
cabin. "Just hearing the smile in your voice is
payment enough."

"Okay, I am smiling, but that's not enough. Alex agrees."

"Are the renovations to your liking?"

"Of course. We love all of it: the tile, vanity, mirror, and thank you for getting rid of that ugly-ass black toilet!"

She hadn't mentioned the washer and dryer, so Jerry took a chance. "Did you see the present I left you in the closet?"

"Oh my God, you bought us a washer and dryer. Alex, come look!"

Jerry laughed. "I needed to do laundry and was too lazy to go to the laundromat."

"Hilarious, but we still need to repay you."

"I'll take it in trade."

"What do you have in mind?"

"I need some information."

"Like?"

"What would make a spirit angry?"

"You mean besides the fact they're a spirit?"

"I'm working with the ghost. She visited Max in her dream, only the next morning, the kid had a bruise."

"Poor kid."

"There's more. The ghost was using Max to get to me. I was having dinner with Max and her mom, and the spirit trapped her in the bathroom. Scared the crap out of her and told her to bring me to her."

"What'd you do?"

"I went. But when I got there, I started by laying down the rules. I told her that she is never to touch Max again."

"What did she say?"

"She disappeared. Then this morning, she was totally different. Cooperative, nice, even her energy was calm. I want to think I got through to her, but I think there's more to it."

"You're probably right. Do you know anything about her death?"

"She was murdered."

"When?"

"August 16."

"No, I mean did she die during the day or at night?"

"Night. That's the guy's MO."

"I'm just reaching, but if she died at night, maybe that is why her energy is so dark at night."

"Sounds like as good a reason as any."

"Wait, you said it is this guy's MO. Are you working on a murder case?"

Jerry knew whatever he said would get back to Alex. Not that he minded; Alex was a good cop and would make an even better detective. "I think it's bigger than that."

"What do you mean?"

"I'm pretty sure this case is connected to my friend's death in Tennessee."

"You're in Michigan, right?"

"Yep."

"So you're talking what, a serial killer?"

"It's still early."

"But that's what you're thinking."

Jerry sighed. "It's my best guess."

"Holy shit!"

"You can tell Alex, but tell her to keep it under wraps until we know more. I don't want to leak anything that might prevent us from nailing this psycho."

"Understood. Now about your payment."

"Just lend me a room from time to time, and we'll call it even. Listen, I've got to go. I'll talk to you soon." Jerry switched off the phone and sat drumming his fingers together. If he was right and Ashley's killer was the same guy who killed Patti, then it would be safe to think he would have disposed of the body the same way. The first thing would be to locate where the body was buried, then try to convince the authorities to act on his hunch, something that would be easier to do if they knew the woman was missing in the first place. Jerry ran his hands through his hair. *Don't get ahead of yourself, McNeal. No body, no crime.*

Chapter Thirteen

Max and April were sitting on the porch steps when Jerry pulled into the driveway. Gunter barked an enthusiastic greeting and moved to the backseat as Max opened the passenger door.

April stepped up to Jerry's window. "So, where are you two off to?"

"Gravedigging."

April raised an eyebrow. "Seriously?"

Jerry shook his head. "Probably not going to do any actual digging, but we need to find where Ashley's body is buried in order to give her peace. You're welcome to come along."

April shook her head. "Thanks, but I have to work. Besides, I'm not a fan of cemeteries."

Jerry turned to Max. "Looks like it's just the three of us, kid."

April looked through the window. "Three of you?"

Jerry jabbed a thumb toward the backseat. "Gunter is in the back."

April nodded her understanding. "I keep forgetting about the dog. But I'm glad to know he's going with you."

133

Jerry put the SUV into reverse. "I'm on the other end of my phone if you need anything."

"Ditto." April took a step back, waving as Jerry backed out of the driveway. She continued to stare as they drove away.

"Your mom's pretty okay."

"Yeah."

"Have you two always been close?"

Max laughed. "No. Not until after we moved here."

"What was the big change?"

"She divorced Randy."

"I take it Randy isn't your father."

Max wrinkled her nose. "No. I never knew my dad. Randy was a jerk. I knew it was a mistake when she said she was going to marry him, but that was before she listened to me."

"How old were you when they got married?"

"Five."

Jerry knew all too well how it felt to know something was going to happen and not have your parents listen to you. Lucky for him, his granny always took his gift seriously. "Yeah, grownups don't tend to listen to kids, especially when it comes to matters of the heart."

Max crossed her arms in front of her. "I may have only been five, but I saw what kind of monster he was. I saw him hitting Mom and hurting her. Oh, he was nice at first, but I saw it."

Jerry pulled into Port Hope Cemetery, drove to the middle, and parked. The moment he shut off the engine, Gunter jumped out, running from row to row, sniffing all the graves.

"What are we doing here?"

"Looking for Ashley's body."

"I thought she said she doesn't know where she's buried."

"She doesn't. Neither do we. That's why this part is up to Gunter." Jerry leaned against the Durango, watching as Gunter continued to investigate. "Remember my friend Patti?"

"Yes."

"I'm going to tell you something, but you can't tell anyone else. Not yet anyway."

"Okay."

"I think the man that killed Patti is the same one that killed Ashley. I think that's why Patti sent me here. I think she knew they were connected. That's why both Patti and Ashley said help us. They weren't talking about you – they were talking about the other girls."

"You mean there's more?"

"If I'm right, and I'm pretty sure I am, then yes, many more."

"That's scary."

"Yes, it is."

Max sighed. "We moved to Port Hope because it was supposed to be safe, but it doesn't feel so safe now that we have a murderer killing all of those people here."

Jerry realized what she'd said and shook his head. "No, you misunderstood. I don't think the murderer lives here. As a matter of fact, I'm confident he does not. This man travels to places and then stalks his victims until he finds a suitable place to kill them."

"That makes me happy."

Her answer surprised him. "Why's that?"

"Because I thought the murderer lived here, and now I know he doesn't. I was pretty scared. I didn't tell Chloe about the murder because I didn't want her to be scared like me. I felt pretty bad because I like it here, and Mom likes it here too. It's much better than when we lived in Detroit. I even have friends. Real friends, but Chloe is my best friend."

Max's journals had alluded to her having trouble in school and getting into fights. "It sounds like you had a tough go of it before."

Max shrugged.

"I'm a pretty good listener, you know."

"It was hard because I was different, only I didn't know I was different. I'd go to school and tell something I knew was going to happen before it happened, and they would accuse me of lying. They'd make fun of me for being a weirdo. And later, some of them thought I was a witch and that I only knew what was going to happen because I was putting a spell on them to make it happen. I got in a lot of fights, some I started, but most were started by others."

"Your mom didn't do anything to help?"

"She tried, but Randy made her stop. He said if I was going to go around making stuff up that I needed to learn to fight my own battles."

"I wish she would have tried harder."

"Don't be mad at her. It's hard to fight someone else's battles when you're getting beat yourself. I didn't understand that at the time, but I do now. Randy used to really beat on her."

Jerry's nostrils flared. "Did he ever touch you?"

"Yes, but not in a bad way. I had a friend whose stepdad did bad things. The only thing Randy ever did was beat me."

That the kid considered herself lucky amazed him. Gunter ran up to Jerry and sat with his tongue hanging out of the side of his mouth. Jerry nodded to Max. "He didn't find anything, so on to the next one."

Max got in and reclined her seat so she could just see out the window. "How does Gunter know what he's looking for?"

Jerry wheeled the Durango around and headed south. "Good question and one I'm not exactly sure of. He seems to know who we are looking for – I told him we're looking for Ashley, and he seems to understand his mission. He found Patti without my asking for his help. I think it is because he's a ghost, like him helping me with other things and protecting you when you were in danger. All I had to do was think that he needed to help you, and he was there. I think it might be one of his gifts."

They checked out two more cemeteries near Harbor Beach and continued south. As they moved south, Jerry began to feel a tingle along the base of his neck. *We're getting closer.* He purposely kept that information to himself, waiting to see if Max would pick up on the pull on her own. He pretended not to notice when she raised in her seat, leaning forward as if responding to the energy. They were closer now, so much so that Gunter was pacing back and forth in the second-row seat. Just as Jerry was about to say something, Max pointed to a road up ahead.

"Good job, Max." Jerry slowed. As he made the turn onto Helena Road, he saw a cemetery to his right. Sitting tucked on top of the hill, he would have missed it if not for the feeling that drew him there. An arched metal sign welcomed them to Saint Anthony, a small uncrowded cemetery that literally sat in the middle of nowhere. While there were some grain bins nearby, the closest house looked to be over half a mile away. Gunter jumped out, sniffing at the headstones even before Jerry shut off the engine. He and Max got out and stood next to the front of the Durango, leaving Gunter room to do his job. Other than a chainsaw in the distance and a few birds hovering overhead, the cemetery was quiet. "Our guy is smart."

"He is?"

"Yep. This is the perfect location. He could have made all the noise he wanted, and most likely, no one would have heard."

Jerry's cell phone rang. He pulled it out, saw it was Seltzer, moved to the side of the vehicle, and answered the call. "Did you find anything?"

"Did I ever. When Ms. Fabel said she was connected, she wasn't lying. Her family is among one of the oldest in Boston. They have ties to politicians and are rumored to be affiliated with the mob. Within moments of running a background check on her, I received a phone call from the family attorney wanting to know why I was looking into his client. Apparently, Ms. Fabel has been known to go underground in the past, and the family was waiting for her to emerge somewhere. The man was very persuasive and let me know the family had placed a sizeable reward for anyone with knowledge of the woman's whereabouts."

Now wearing his K-9 police vest, Gunter had keyed upon a headstone and was currently staring at Jerry as if willing him to come see what he'd found. "Did he say whether the reward would be awarded if the woman was no longer with us?"

"I take it you found the body."

"Looking like it. Now to figure out how to convince the authorities to dig up a grave to find a woman they don't know is missing."

The squeak on the other end of the line let Jerry know that Seltzer had leaned back in his chair – most likely while chewing on two sticks of his favorite chewing gum. "I don't see that being a problem."

"Why's that?"

"As we speak, Mario Fabel and his attorney are onboard a private jet heading to the closest airport to your location, which by my calculations is one Sandusky, Michigan, and should take about ninety minutes of airtime."

Jerry laughed. "I doubt Mr. Fabel will have much success finding a rental car around here."

"From what I can ascertain, Mr. Fabel doesn't have trouble getting anything he sets his mind to."

Jerry looked over at Max. "Good. The sooner Ashley is rejoined with her family, the better for everyone involved."

"Understood. I gave Mr. Fabel's attorney your number. He will make contact when they make it to the area."

"You're telling me you wouldn't give my number to a hot chick, but you gave it to a person who could disappear me with no one knowing?"

"The guy was very persuasive."

"How persuasive?"

"He knew about the lengths I've taken to get you

out of trouble over the last few months."

"That means he has people on the inside."

"As I said, Ms. Fabel wasn't lying when she told you she was connected. Watch your back, McNeal."

"My back, my front, and every other part of me." Jerry hung up the phone and turned to face Max. "It appears Gunter found what he was looking for."

They walked over to the grave, where Gunter stood guard. The headstone displayed the last name Willis along with the date August 14, 2019. *Six years*. Jerry ruffled the dog's fur. "Good boy, Gunter."

"But it's the wrong date. Ashley said he killed her on August 16."

"You're right, but the guy would have most likely searched the obits looking for a freshly dug grave. That way, his digging wouldn't raise suspicion."

"So now we dig?"

"Nope. We found where she's buried, so our job is pretty much done. Now it will be up to the authorities to get permission to dig."

"It's that easy?"

"Not usually, but apparently, Ms. Ashley has friends on the way that will see to things."

Max didn't answer.

Jerry looked and noticed the color had drained from her face. "You okay there, kid?"

Max blinked back tears as she struggled to find

her words. "Jerry, you're covered in blood."

Jerry looked down then back at Max. "No, I'm not."

"But you were just a second ago. It's going to happen. I saw it!"

Jerry worked to sound calm. "Do you see anything else?"

"Just that you're on your knees covered in blood."

"And your premonitions always come true?"

Tears trailed down her cheeks as she wordlessly nodded her head.

Jerry knew he had stood far enough away that Max couldn't have overheard his conversation with Seltzer. He forced a smile and ran a hand over his head to ease his nerves. "I guess we'd better get you home then."

Chapter Fourteen

Jerry followed behind Max and Gunter, wondering about his next play. The pistol in his waistband gave little comfort, given Max's premonition saw him covered in blood. He watched as she climbed into the passenger seat of the Durango. First things first, get the girl home.

Jerry had no sooner finished the thought than the hairs on the back of his neck began to prickle. He pulled his pistol and scanned the area. Nothing. *Easy, McNeal, you're acting like a spooked rabbit.* Jerry returned his gun to his waistband.

Gunter barked, ran past him, then took off down Helena Road. The dog was too fast to follow, and Jerry had no intention of leaving Max unprotected, so he climbed inside the Durango and followed.

Max scooted forward in her seat. "Where's he going?"

"Your guess is as good as mine, but something's up. Gunter still has his vest on, and the hair on the back of my neck is crawling." Jerry came to a rolling stop at M25, looked both ways, then continued straight on Helena driving slow, looking for signs of Gunter.

"I feel someone calling for help."

Jerry barely touched the gas pedal as he crept along the road watching for Gunter. "These calls. Do they sound desperate or single calls for help?"

"I don't know. Does it matter?"

Jerry glanced in her direction. "I heard a chainsaw earlier."

"Oh my God, do you think…"

Yep. Jerry shrugged. "I don't hear the chainsaw now."

"Maybe whoever it was…why are you speeding up? Did you hear something?"

Actually, he saw something – Gunter standing in the middle of the road covered in blood. When the dog saw he had Jerry's attention, the blood faded as he took off running up a cleared path. Jerry straddled the small ditch with the Durango, got out, and tossed his cell phone to Max. "Call 911."

"I don't hear anything."

"Make the call! Tell them we are on Helena Road, there's been an accident, and to send an ambulance." Jerry followed Gunter through a freshly cleared path, where he found a man slumped near the base of a tree, covered in blood. Though he knew there'd been an accident, Jerry wasn't prepared for the sight of so much blood.

Instantly, he was with his Marine unit looking down at Johnson, whose leg had nearly been severed by an IED. Jerry's heart pounded in his chest as he took in all the blood. *Shit!* Jerry ran a hand over his head. He'd known something was going to happen the moment they'd started out. He'd tried to warn the sergeant, but they'd received orders on where to patrol. Since Jerry only had a feeling and couldn't provide any solid details, the man wouldn't budge. Johnson had led the patrol and tripped the IED.

Do something, McNeal. You can't let the man die. Jerry searched the woods. Funny, he hadn't remembered being in the woods. *Where's Doc?*

Suddenly, something hit him square in the chest. Jerry blinked and was instantly brought back to the present when he saw that something to be the solid paws of his ghostly companion who'd jumped up, placing his front paws on Jerry's chest.

Jerry pushed Gunter aside and dropped to his knees. The blood came from a single wound, a deep gash that ran the width of the man's upper right thigh. "Sir, can you hear me?"

No answer.

Jerry checked the guy for a belt, pulled it loose, and used it to make a tourniquet a few inches above the wound. Once he'd controlled the bleeding, he checked the man's pulse. Slow, but it was there. Jerry pulled his shirt over his head and placed it on the wound, holding pressure to further ease the blood flow.

The man's eyes fluttered.

"Sir? I need you to stay with me."

Jerry's hand was still tender from the run-in with both the mirror and door. He felt it begin to throb. *Shit. Where the hell is she?*

He looked to Gunter. "Go get Max!"

Gunter barked and took off running. A couple of minutes later, Jerry looked up to see them both running down the path.

Max's shirt was covered in dirt, and her hair was disheveled, so much so, Jerry wondered if she'd fallen. She neared, saw the blood, and her face paled. "Jerry, it's my vision. You're covered in blood."

Well, that's a relief.

"Is he alive?"

"For now." Jerry threw her his key. "Go back to the Durango. There's a blanket and first aid kit in the back."

Max stood frozen in place as if mesmerized by the sight of the blood.

"Go!" Jerry understood her hesitation, but his own flashback had already wasted precious time. Max took off running, and Gunter stood looking from Jerry to the path as if trying to decide where he was needed. Jerry gave the nod. "Go with Max."

Gunter barked and tore off after her.

Jerry turned his attention to the man, who looked to be in his mid to late sixties. "Sir, I'm Trooper McNeal," *Where did that come from?* It had been months since he'd been on the job. *Focus, McNeal, you can iron out the details later.* "Can you tell me your name?"

The man moaned and mumbled something Jerry couldn't decipher. "Come on, sir. I need you to stay with me. What's your name?"

The man's eyes fluttered.

"That's it. Stay with me. What's your name?"

The man's words came out in a jumbled mess.

"I didn't get that. Come on, sir. Tell me your name."

"Arnold."

"Good. Okay, Arnold, do you have a last name?" Of course, he did, but Jerry needed to keep him talking.

"Davies."

"Okay, Mr. Davies, we called for help. You hang in there, now." It seemed like an eternity before Max returned. Jerry's hand throbbed, but he'd managed to keep Arnold awake and from losing any more blood.

Max approached without hesitation. Her color was back, and she seemed to have recovered from her initial shock. "I have the blanket and first aid kit."

Jerry nodded to the kit. "Grab me some gauze."

Max tore into several packs and handed them to Jerry, who placed them on top of his blood-soaked shirt. Jerry nodded to the man's leg. "I need you to loosen the belt just a bit."

Max took a step back. "I'm not good with

blood."

"Get good!" *Shit!* Jerry took in a breath and lowered his tone. "He's lost a lot of blood. You listen to me, and Arnold here has a good chance at staying alive."

She swallowed, nodded her agreement, and slipped on a pair of rubber gloves. "Okay."

"That's a girl." Keeping pressure on Arnold's leg, he moved to the side. "Now loosen the belt...not too much now."

Max worked at the belt, and Arnold moaned. "I'm hurting him."

"Come on, Max, stay with me. You're doing great."

Her mouth trembled as she worked the belt loose.

"That's it. Good, now buckle it." Jerry waited until she'd done as he said, then slowly released the pressure on the wound, breathing a sigh of relief when he didn't see any fresh blood seeping from under the gauze. He flexed his hand and continued with the pressure.

She looked at him expectantly. "Now what?"

"Now we wait for the cavalry." Jerry smiled. "You did good, Max. Your mom is going to be so proud."

"I pulled a small tree over the road to show where we were. I guess someone could move it before they arrive. Maybe I should go to the road and wait for the police."

That explains her appearance. Jerry gave a slight nod to Gunter, who took off up the path. "Nah, you told them what road we are on, and the Durango is parked there. They'll find us."

"You looked scared when I told you about my vision. I'm glad it wasn't your blood."

Before he could answer, sirens blared in the distance, followed by Gunter's eager barks. Max smiled. "They're coming."

***

Jerry was parked in front of the camper loading his belongings into the Durango when Gunter growled a deep growl. He heard gravel crunch under the wheels of a car and knew without looking Fabel had arrived. A car door opened and shut, again with the crunching gravel and the click of a second door. A man that had a private jet at his disposal and was accustomed to having doors opened for him wasn't the kind of man who did his own dirty work. Jerry slid the secondary pistol under the seat and closed the door as he turned.

With dark hair, a tailored black suit, and designer sunglasses, Mario Fabel looked as if he'd just stepped out of a mafia movie. His driver, on the other hand, would have been right at home in the *Soldier of Fortune* magazine. A third man getting out on the other side wielding a briefcase looked like the lawyer Jerry assumed him to be. Mario surveyed the campsite, saw Mr. Mills sitting in his Adirondack chair with a newspaper folded in his lap, and nodded toward the camper. "Can we speak inside?"

Jerry cast a glance at Mills, then at the driver. "You and your lawyer can come in. That one stays outside."

The edges of Mario's lips curled. "Agreed."

Jerry motioned the men to the couch and took a seat in the recliner across the room, careful not to upset the shotgun leaning against the wall behind the chair. Gunter took up a position directly in front of Jerry.

Fabel considered Jerry for a moment. "You're not a very trusting sort, are you?"

Jerry met the man's stare. "I doubt you traveled all this way to discuss my personality traits."

A pained look crossed the man's face. "No, I came to collect my sister."

"I won't bother to ask how you were able to attend to the task so quickly."

"We all have our talents, Mr. McNeal."

"So, if you have what you came for, why the need for a visit?"

"Isn't it enough that I wanted to give my thanks to the man who found my sister?"

"It would be if that was the reason you came."

"Touché."

"I'll ask again, why are you here?"

"I wanted to meet the man who did what no one else could. I have what some would deem unlimited resources, Mr. McNeal. My sister has been missing for four years. In that time, none of my associates have been able to locate her – I'm saying not so much as a whisper. And you are not only able to find her, but tell me where to find the body. You must know there is a sizable reward on the table. Money that might look inviting to a man such as yourself with no job."

Jerry laced his hands together and leaned forward in his chair. "Are you accusing me of killing your sister?"

Mario mirrored Jerry. "If I thought that were the case, there would be no need for discussion. What I want to know is how."

Jerry leaned back in his chair and echoed Fabel's words. "We all have our talents, Mr. Fabel."

Fabel sighed and jutted a chin toward the attorney, who remained silent. The attorney placed his briefcase on his lap and opened it. While Jerry couldn't see what was inside, he could judge the man's body language, which did not appear threatening. The man reached inside the case and then placed three large stacks of large bills on the table in front of him.

Jerry eyed the money, then looked at Fabel. "I told you I was not interested in your money."

Fabel's brow arched. "The money isn't for you,

Mr. McNeal. It is for the girl and her mother."

Shit. He'd thought he would be able to keep Max and April out of this.

"I did my homework, Mr. McNeal. I know the only reason you are here is that the girl's mother asked you to come. I also know neither of them is responsible for my sister's death. What I do know is I am a man of my word, and this money would be a welcome windfall for them and would afford Max an extended education she might otherwise not be privileged to receive. Surely you would not object to my seeing them looked after?"

How could he argue with that? "I do not."

"The money comes with my word that if they ever find themselves needing an attorney, Mr. Brinkley here will see to the matter himself. It has also come to my attention that you and Sergeant Seltzer also have some rather dubious dealings in regard to the law, so since you will not accept payment for your part, I will extend Mr. Brinkley's services to the two of you as well. I assure you the man is most studious in his proceedings."

Brinkley placed several business cards on the cash and closed his briefcase. Both men stood and walked to the door. While Brinkley left, Fabel paused in the doorway. "Since I can't persuade you to tell me your secrets, I will bid you farewell. I'm sure that pistol Mr. Mills holds under his newspaper is getting rather heavy about now."

Jerry followed them out, waited for them to leave, and walked over to Mills, who handed him the pistol. "You doing okay there, Mr. Mills?"

The man smiled. "I haven't felt this alive in years."

Jerry smiled, dropped the magazine, and cleared the weapon, placing the bullet in his pocket. "I'm going to leave you with my number. If that dog of yours ever has puppies, I want you to give me a call. I have a few people on my list that would like to have one."

"Would you be one of them?"

Jerry shook his head. "No, sir, I've never been much of a dog man."

From somewhere close behind, Jerry heard Gunter growl.

Join Jerry McNeal and his ghostly K-9 partner as they put their gifts to good use!:

Now available for preorder:

Cold Case – book 6 in The Jerry McNeal Series
https://www.amazon.com/dp/B09XKLPTC7

Wicked Winds – book 7 in The Jerry McNeal Series
https://www.amazon.com/dp/B0B1H31G86

And, coming Spring of 2023, join Jerry and Gunter as they travel to Deadwood to see Jonesy and a lively cast of spirits in *Spirit of Deadwood*, a fun filled, full-length Jerry McNeal novel.
https://www.amazon.com/dp/B0B1C9XKX7

About the Author

Born in Kentucky, Sherry got her start in writing by pledging to write a happy ending to a good friend who was going through some really tough times. The story surprised her by taking over and practically writing itself. What started off as a way to make her friend smile started her on a journey that would forever change her life. Sherry readily admits to hearing voices and is convinced that being married to her best friend for forty-one-plus years goes a long way in helping her write happily-ever-afters.

Sherry resides in Michigan and spends most of her time writing from her home office, traveling to book signing events, and giving lectures on the Orphan Trains.

Made in the USA
Columbia, SC
24 July 2022

63946328R00089